Raised Catholic

ED STIVENDER

August House Publishers, Inc.
L I T T L E   R O C K

Printed in the United States of America

10 9 8 7 6 5 4   HC
10 9 8 7 6 5 4 3 2   PB

LIBRARY OF CONGRESS CATALOGING-IN-PUBLICATION DATA

Stivender, Ed, 1946–
Raised Catholic: can you tell? / Ed Stivender.
  p.   cm.
ISBN 0-87483-277-2 (hb)
ISBN 0-87483-336-1 (pb)
1. Stivender, Ed, 1946–
2. Catholics—United States—Biography. I. Title.
BX4705.S8264A3   1992
282'.092—dc20   92-19500

First Edition, 1992
First Paperback Edition, 1994

Executive editor: Liz Parkhurst
Editorial assistant: Sue Williams
Design director: Ted Parkhurst
Cover photograph: Seymour Mednick
Cover design: Harvill Ross Studios Ltd.
Typography: Lettergraphics / Little Rock

This book is printed on archival-quality paper which meets the
guidelines for performance and durability of the Committee on
Production Guidelines for Book Longevity of the
Council on Library Resources.

AUGUST HOUSE, INC.   PUBLISHERS   LITTLE ROCK

stories about my Catholic boyhood in performance. A year later, we did a concert together at the Great Lakes Pastoral Gathering in Chicago, produced by Loretta Reif. The "Altar Boy" and "Diane Tasca" stories appeared at that time, though in a different form.

I would never have met Jim May if Jimmy Neil Smith had not invented the Bugaboo Springs (now National) Storytelling Festival in Jonesborough, Tennessee, sparking a revival which brought Connie Regan–Blake and Barbara Freeman, missionaries extraordinaire, to Hartford, Connecticut, beating the bushes for working performers.

I would not have been a working storyteller if it had not been for the Plum Cake Players and co-founders Tony Wilusz and Regina Mocey, persuading me to leave my teaching job in West Hartford and join them in 1975.

Nor would I have met Jim May were it not for my mentor Jay O'Callahan developing the Washington College Conference so vital to the networking that took place in the early eighties. To all these people, most raised Catholic themselves, I owe a debt of gratitude.

I would also like to thank the people who made this project possible—Nancy Clancy (née Stivender), my manager and organizer, who has helped me since she taught me to tie my shoes when I was six, and whose handling of my schedule and arrangements has kept me working and solvent for the past decade; Liz Parkhurst, the editor of this book, whose well-timed encouragements and corrections have made the experience rational and almost fun; Donald Davis, pioneer of this process of putting performance on paper; and Diane Wolkstein, who dared me to go through with it.

Thanks to the storytelling communities that have provided a context for my work over the last two decades—the Blue Mountain Group, Patchwork of Philadelphia, as well as the casual structures of colleagues and friends whose influence will be clear in these pages.

My classmates at Holy Cross and Bonner High School need to be acknowledged for providing the matrix of these stories. Some are mentioned by name, some in code, all are remembered with fondness. Mike Miscio taught me about rapport.

I hope that members of my family will not accuse me of taking their names in vain, or misrepresenting them. My sister Karen was born after most of the events these stories are based on and will have to wait for my next book. The same goes for the Epprights and McGarveys. My Aunt Bet, my family's Aunt Spooky, was an important influence on my early days, but also is given short shrift. My cousin Tom wasn't really the crybaby he seems to be here.

Finally, I'd like to thank the Sisters of Mercy who taught me at Holy Cross Elementary School, especially Sister Virginia Mary, R.S.M., who set the tone of my entire education, and Sister Patrick Mary, R.S.M., who put me on stage for the first time. ❧

ly, it might have seemed inevitable. I was the firstborn son of an Irish Catholic mother and had excellent reading and memorization skills. As the winner of General Excellence and Religion awards at Holy Cross Elementary School, an altar boy, Lieutenant of the Safeties, and First Class Scout, I was a prime candidate for the seminary and was made to feel by all the nuns who taught me that I did have a vocation.

In the Early Church, by which I mean the period from the Council of Jerusalem until 1965 A.D., when the reforms of Vatican II began to seep into the language of the priests of the Philadelphia Archdiocese, the word *vocation* meant one thing, and one thing only: the call to the priesthood, if you were a boy who was smart enough, or to the religious life—a convent or monastery—if you were a girl, or a devout boy with low test scores.

My test scores were high enough. The only problem was that I never heard a call. The nuns had warned us that it wasn't necessarily an audible message that you received, but I held out for a long time, hung on the horns of the dilemma of celibacy, waiting for the call. In the meantime, I took a degree in English with the Jesuits at St. Joseph's College, becoming a contentious debater in the required eighty hours of Philosophy and Theology. I even interviewed with the Discalced Carmelites in my senior year but went to Notre

Dame instead to study theology, while my draft board discussed my status as a lay Catholic pacifist. I never heard a call to the priesthood.

I did hear a call, though, in 1974. Waking up from a nap on Martha's Vineyard, I distinctly heard the word *dancer*. It was certainly too late by then to start the training necessary to become a Nureyev or Gene Kelly, but it did crystallize a self-image implicit since I had won my fifth-grade dance contest.

Genetically, this vocation might have seemed inevitable. My parents danced often in the living room as I was growing up. My mother taught me the jitterbug when I was eight or so. My father was the hit of every party he ever went to because of his smooth moves. And if there is a legacy he left me, it is the honor and duty of a dancing man to draw the flowers off the wall at wedding receptions and tense social events and swing or sway them through the space.

In ancient Rome there was an order of priest-dancers called the Salii, who would go out on the first of the year and dance and leap in honor of their patron, Mars. If I had been living in that time, I would probably be agonizing with my scribe as to why I did not become a member of this order.

In this book of stories there are several moments of dancing, and in the writing of it dancing has been an important device. I have danced around issues of privacy and pain, propriety and pleasure. My fingers have danced on the keys of a Royal 440 that is propped up on two volumes of the OED, enabling me to stand as I write, getting me as close as possible to the sometimes subtle, sometimes frantic dance I do before a microphone in my work as a performing storyteller.

And so I say to my Lutheran father, Alvey Stivender, "Here I dance, I can do no other." And to you, with the eyes, "Come dance with me."

—*Ed Stivender*
PHILADELPHIA

Guardian Angel

*F*or my sixth birthday I received school supplies in preparation for my entrance into the Holy Cross Elementary School, which was to come a week later. My presents included a plaid, buckle-flap bookbag with both handle and strap; two notebooks—one marble-covered with units and measures on the back, the other small and spiral-bound for writing homework assignments; a pencil case with a clear blue Scripto lead pencil with lead storage space, as well as a two-tone red/blue pencil and a large eraser. I was well equipped for the adventure to come.

Two weeks earlier my father had taken me to the shopping district at the end of the suburban bus line to have me fitted for the uniform I would wear versions of for the next eight years—gray pants, maroon blazer, black shoes, white shirt, and necktie. On the pocket of the blazer my mother had sewn a patch of the school shield—a gold embroidered HC. A haircut on the Friday before Labor Day was the finishing touch. I was ready to begin my training as a young Catholic Gentleman.

My Protestant father had set the wheels in motion seven years earlier when he signed a paper turning over his rights to educate his future children to the Catholic church. This was a prerequisite to marrying my mother, and a small price to pay for love.

My education as a Catholic had started long before now, however. I had been going to church with my mother since my baptism, and had learned to recite the Hail Mary and most of the Our Father. I knew how to bless myself and genuflect and take off my hat in church. I was primed for this moment.

Holy Cross Parish existed before any buildings were erected on its ten acres. The property had been bought by the Archdiocese of Philadelphia in response to the postwar housing developments erected on the farm land on the other side of Darby Creek. The farmhouse itself would become the rectory for Father Louis J. Meyer, chaplain in the U.S. Army and pastor of the flock of newly married veterans and their wives who would produce the Baby Boom necessitating the building of a school—even before a church was thought of. Mass in the early days was celebrated in the Fire Hall out Bishop Road on U.S. Route 1.

The original parish boundaries included Westbrook Park—row houses that could be purchased for less than ten thousand dollars—and Colonial Park—detached houses that were more expensive. The Catholic children from these two new neighborhoods populated the new school, and Mass was said in the all-purpose assembly hall that graced the top of the hill, when the hall was finally built. But first there was the school, and the convent.

The school was constructed in a simple style—brick exterior, painted cinder block interior, wooden floors in the classrooms, composite stone in the corridors. Surrounding the building was a vast playground of macadam that would have been used as a parking lot, except that parishioners were expected to walk to Mass.

On the first day of school, the children who were destined for first grade gathered in this pl----

parents. Th--

---- ---- eyebrows.

---- ---- silent, a few children cried louder, jumping into their parents' arms. Near the edge of the group, someone vomited. I was thankful it wasn't me.

"Good morning, children, parents," said the imposing figure in a strong clear voice. "I am going to call the roll and you will please line up without your parents as you hear your name. Joanna Appel, Joseph Asher, Patricia Boyce ..."

Since my last name was Stivender, I would be called near the end, and so I had a chance to watch several tearful farewells before it was my turn to line up. When my name was called, I kissed my mother gently on the cheek and took my place, scared of what lay within the double doors at the nun's back but ready to face it.

"Now, children, we will go through the doors. Turn right and walk silently down the corridor to the end room on the right," she announced.

We obeyed, most of us. The vomiter and one or two other panic-stricken students would join us later in the week.

As we entered the classroom I noticed that we would be sitting two to a desk. One hundred and eight of us, fifty-four desks. I took my seat next to Mary Beth Sweeney, daughter of the undertaker on Baltimore Pike. She was cute, and though her hair was made up like Judy Garland's in *The*

Wizard of Oz, I knew we weren't in Kansas anymore. A woman in black held us captive.

When we were all seated, Sister taught us the first rule of Catholic Education. "Now, children, make sure there is room for your Guardian Angel between you and your seat partner." I squirmed away from Mary Beth, as she did from me, which wasn't hard since everyone knew that members of the opposite sex had "cooties." I was somewhat familiar with the concept of a Guardian Angel from pictures depicting a child on a dangerous precipice with a gentle robed asexual blond-haired figure with wings hovering over for protection. Leaving room for such a figure between myself and another person was new to me, however. Eight years or so later at Catholic Teen dances the concept would again be introduced as a way of preventing the untoward touching associated with doing "the Grind," or "Dirty Dig." Chaperons would roam the floor, tapping couples on the shoulder and reminding them of the idea. But on this day my mind tried to imagine how two Guardian Angels would fare in the same space, separating their respective wards. I supposed they just squeezed in between us.

"Now fold your hands and put them, folded, on the edge of the desk," she continued, demonstrating with her own hands the interlocking of the fingers. I obeyed, right pinky finger becoming dented by the corner of the desk top, starting the callous that would continue through grade school.

The desk was made of wood bolted on cast iron which was then bolted to wooden runners. Below the writing surface was a space for books which could be seen through the cast-iron filigree of grape leaves and vines. Drilled into the top surface was a hole meant for inkwells, now empty, and a cleft to hold pencils. The writing surface held shadows of names and dates cut in, then sanded down and shellacked over.

"Now, children, look up here on the blackboard and I will write my name."

She did so, then stood back and picked up a long varnished stick with an eye-scre~~

~~ ~ ~

~~ ~~~~~~ along. A hand

~~ ~~~ up in the first row.

Sister checked a chart on her desk and called on the hand-raiser by name, "Master Asher?" This was the first time I had heard such a title. It would not be the last. The girls would be addressed as "Miss." Catholic school was a very formal place.

"Is Mary your last name?" Joseph Asher asked, innocently. No one laughed. We wouldn't have dared, even if we had seen the humor of the question, which we didn't.

"No, Master Asher, I am a Sister of Mercy, and when we join our order, we take new names and give up our family names. We all have Mary somewhere in our new names, however, so it's *almost* a last name. We also give up our birthdays and instead celebrate the feast day of the person whose name we take."

I would realize later the Sister Virginia Mary had chosen her name wisely. Sister Mary Patrice, the principal, would celebrate her feast day on March 17, Sister Edward Mary on October 13, and so on, but by taking the name of the Virgin Mother of God, Sister Virginia Mary had ensured recognition for herself on the day of all of the feasts of the Virgin, which were plentiful, including the entire month of May.

"Now, children, I am going to take the roll. When I call your name, I want you to stand next to your seat, and bow if you are a boy," she said, demonstrating this gesture, "or curtsey if you are a girl"—again, demonstrating—"and say in a clear voice, 'Present, Sister.'"

"Joanna Appel."

The first girl in the first row stood, curtseyed, said, "Present, Sister," and sat down again. As the roll continued, I looked around the room. There were long slate blackboards on the front and side walls. Connected to these were cork bulletin boards with cheerful back-to-school pictures and renderings of saints. Above the boards were large flash cards with letters written in what I would later learn was the Palmer Method. I recognized most of the letters, the others I could figure out from context and position, the most interesting being the Q, the capital was written like a graceful number two and the small letter (lower case we would call it today) looked a lot like the *p*. Sister's handwriting was exactly like the letters above. At the beginning of the alphabet were cards with a series of O's, like a sideways tornado, and zigzags. Within the week, we would learn to duplicate these cards on paper as a preliminary step toward writing.

"Dennis Coneen ..." continued Sister, her eye on the class daunting potential fidgeters.

My eyes wandered to the crucifix above the front board. It was a fine one, with a real wooden cross and well-painted corpus. Above the side board was a cloth-covered box that we would learn later held the speaker of the PA system. These two items—crucifix and PA speaker—would be constant in every Catholic classroom I would attend for the next twelve years.

"Joseph Keohane ..."

I had plenty of time before my turn to rise. Near the front door there was a closet in which were kept the supplies and tools to be used throughout the year—boxes of giant no-roll crayons, reams of paper with double and dotted lines for penmanship, maps, a large broom, small broom, dustpan and brush, as well as boxes of books provided by the archdiocese.

"Michael Menseck "

, records of absence, and other administrative forms.

"Thomas O'Leary ..."

Having the last initial of *S* in my name would mean a seat by the window for most of my school career, allowing me a potential for daydreaming denied my lower-alphabetical peers. This window looked out onto the schoolyard and the grove of white birches beyond, and afforded me a full view of the sky. In later years I would scan this same sky for incoming Communist MIGs carrying atomic bombs, but today there was no such threat.

"Constance Scally ..."

Constance, two seats ahead, was up and curtseying. I prepared myself for my turn. *Present Sister, Present Sister,* I whispered to myself, wanting to make good on the first day. Closer and closer.

"Edward Stivender."

I stood, knees shaking, placed one arm across my waist, the other behind my back, bowed low, and said, "Pressure, System." There was a hush followed by scatterings of laughter. I sat down and looked up at the nun. Her face was immobile. She cleared her throat and went on. "Mary Beth Sweeney." The moment of horror passed. Sister Virginia Mary was the first of many to overlook one of my mistakes in the interest of order and mercy. I was grateful.

When she had finished the roll, she said, "Very good children, you all can bow and curtsey well. Next we are going to try it together. Whenever a sister or a priest comes into the classroom you are to stop whatever you are doing, rise from your seat, bow or curtsey, and say 'Good Morning, Father Meyer'—or whoever it might be—and then stand until they tell you to be seated. Let's try it. I'll come in."

She went out the door for half a second and returned. We rose as best we could, the inner aisles being twice as crowded as my window aisle. After a few tries we had the knack and had developed a singsong style that would stay with us forever. Even today I am tempted to rise and bow when a priest or nun enters a room where I am seated.

We didn't have long to wait to try out our new skill. We heard a knock on the door, and Sister nodded to Joanna Appel, who rose quickly to open it. (This job always went to the first person alphabetically, the only real advantage of having your last name begin with *A*.)

In stepped another person in a black robe, this time a stern-looking man with a burr haircut and a military manner—the pastor, Father Meyer. We all rose and jostled, bowed and chanted, "Good morning, Father"—"Meyer," Sister cued us—"Meyer."

"Good morning, children," said the priest. "Please be seated." We all jostled back. Some students accidently touched their seatmates then moved quickly away, remembering their Guardian Angels.

Sister spoke. "Children, this is the pastor of Holy Cross Parish. Where have you seen him before?"

A hand or two went up. "Miss Watson?"

"I've seen him at church on Sunday."

"That's right. Welcome to our classroom, Father Meyer, may I introduce the first-grade class."

"Yes, and a fine group they are, Sister."

"Would you like to say a few words to the class, Father?" said Sister, moving away from the front of the classroom toward the window aisle to give him the floor.

Father Meyer began to say a few words about being good and obedient, but I can't say I really listened, transfixed as I was by the vision slowly moving toward us S's, T's and W's by the window, giving me a chance to see her clothing

dress around her face. The veil she wore stayed magically on her headpiece and came down past her shoulders, down her back in folds. It looked a lot like the veil of the Blessed Mother in the pictures and statues. In fact, *she* looked a lot like the Blessed Mother, only taller. She looked at me and frowned because I wasn't paying attention. I quickly lowered my eyes and looked at her beautiful black leather shoes as they silently squeaked down the waxed wood floors. As she passed slowly on her way to the back of the room, I caught her scent. It was the most wonderful scent of a woman I had ever smelled. No perfume, no deodorant, no hairspray, not even talcum powder. A slight tinge of starch, but mostly just Ivory soap. She smelled holy, not incense and candle holy, but human holy. What the Blessed Mother must have smelled like.

And so began my secret chaste and courtly love for my first-grade nun, which would vicariously extend to other Mercy nuns with whom I would spend my school days over the next eight years. And beyond. Until the reforms of Vatican II let them put aside their veils, bibs, and wimples, and become human like everybody else.

The vision having passed down the aisle to the back of the room, I was able to refocus on the pastor.

"Now you don't want to become one of those High-IQ Boys who are too smart for their own good." This would be a recurring theme of Father Meyer throughout my experience with him, that being smart was not the greatest value, in fact it could really hurt you. What one should strive for was to be a hard worker, honest, thrifty, helpful, trustworthy, obedient, respectful of grownups, especially priests or nuns—in short, worthy of the Irish puritan work ethic that made America the promised land it was.

"... In fact what you are going to be trained to be here at Holy Cross are Good Christian Gentlemen and Ladies. If Sister needs a helping hand, you'll be there. If she needs help cleaning the classroom after school, you'll be there. If she drops her chalk, you'll pick it up. If she needs a door opened, you'll open it. If she has a package, you'll help her carry it, help her carry her books." I began to listen intently as he outlined a code of action that I would follow for the next several years.

It would not be difficult, since most of these values, military as they were, were the same as those I was learning at home, my father being a Navy man and all. I was determined to be the best darn parochial school student Holy Cross had ever had. It was perfect; by being a good student in the extended family that was the Catholic School of the 1950s, I could be a good son to my immediate family. This was fun.

Father finished his presentation, and then said, "Now kneel down, children, and I'll give you my blessing." This was something we were not prepared for. We all jostled out of our seats and tried to kneel down without kneeling on our neighbor's calves. Near the window it was not so difficult, since there was no opposing row to compensate for, but in the middle of the class, the jostling was becoming an uproar, and two aisles away the situation was becoming serious as students were falling like dominos, crushing one another as they fell.

Sister Virginia Mary spoke over the noise, "I think, Father, they might receive your blessing seated today. Children, sit down in your seats." From the back of the room she began to help the fallen children, comforting a few

...ing that Father Meyer said, and figure out a way to do it."

Easy for me. I had done my homework already. Tomorrow I would help Sister carry her bag from the convent to the school. Being a Christian Gentleman was going to be easy.

Early the next morning I took my place on the sidewalk leading to the convent, at the spot every nun would have to pass just a few yards across a macadam driveway. As I waited in ambush, I rehearsed my line—the six magic words that would ensure my success in Catholic school—"Sister, may I carry your bag?"

I waited there as the convent door opened several times, releasing other sisters to whom I nodded and greeted with "Good morning, Sister." Finally Sister Virginia Mary came down the sidewalk. I ran up to her and offered my assistance.

"Thank you, young man, you are ..."

"Edward Stivender, Sister."

"Well, Master Stivender, you're here early this morning."

"Yes, Sister, trying to do my homework—you know, take one of the things Father mentioned and do it."

"Oh, I see, well this bag is a little heavy."

"Don't worry, I can do it," I said hopefully.

The bookbags that the Mercy nuns carried were black leather accordion-expansion cases that hinged at the top and were held closed by a brass clasp with a lock. I was about to discover that it was not so much a question of carrying it as of dragging it. But I was determined. She placed the bag on the ground in front of me, and with both hands I lifted it and, positioning it against my hip, limped across the drive and into the school. I huffed and puffed down the steps to the ground floor. The long corridor loomed before me.

"I'll go ahead and open the room," she said, her rosary rattling as she increased her pace. It didn't occur to me that it was she who was doing the favor, as is often the case, I have discovered since, with self-appointed helpers and their kidnapped helpees. As I struggled, she unlocked the door and entered the room. I set down the bag in the corridor to take a breath, then resumed my task, arriving in the doorway gasping but successful.

"Put it down by the closet there," she said mercifully, "and go get a drink of water."

"Yes, Sister," I panted. I walked down the corridor to the ceramic water fountain and drank.

As I returned to the classroom I saw some students gathering in the doorway outside. Though the doors would not open until ten after eight, I was inside, privileged because of my helpful attitude. This helpful attitude would become suspect in the older grades, when being a teacher's pet would become unseemly, but for a first-grader it was appropriate.

I returned to the classroom and stood on the threshold. Sister had moved her bag to the desk and was taking books out of it. She looked up.

"Would you like to open the windows?"

Would I? Absolutely yes. I went over and began to open each window, standing on tiptoe to grasp the handle and pull it toward me, unlocking it and hinging the window open. The sounds of the children gathering on the playground filled the room. I could see some of the other kids standing with their parents, waiting for the bell to announce that the doors were open and the students could file in silently.

"I'm going outside..."

graders leaving their parents in the schoolyard. Soon the classroom was full, Mary Beth Sweeney and our Guardian Angels sharing my seat.

That day we learned to stand and pledge allegiance to the flag with our right hand over our hearts, and to bless ourselves, again with the right hand. To this day I know my right from my left from the technique of these gestures. We also began to learn how to write, again with our right hands. I was probably left-handed until then, I still throw with my left. On that day, however, the homogenization process began that resulted in my current ambidexterity.

Sister passed out papers with solid and dotted lines, as well as pencils for those who needed them (not me). Then she took a piece of chalk from a green and white box and approached the blackboard, saying, "Children, take your pencil in your right hand. Good. Now, at the top of the page, in the middle, put a cross, like this."

She drew a simple cross, followed by a dot, as though the cross were a sentence that needed a period. We followed her directions to the best of our abilities. Later on in my education, different teachers would have us write different things at the top of the page, *J.M.J.*, for instance, for "Jesus, Mary and Joseph," or *A.M.D.G.*, the Jesuits' favorite, for the Latin words meaning "For the Greater Glory of God." These notations would presumably bless our work.

"Does everyone have that so far?"

"Yes, Sister."

She drew two parallel lines on the board and began to draw circles between them, like the one on the flash card above the board, and instructed us to do the same, being sure to keep within the lines.

It was harder than it sounds. All of us by that time had had experience with crayons and the line rule, but this was different, more precise, the motor skill necessary was more exact than that demanded by coloring books. She moved up and down the aisles, encouraging us, guiding some of our hands with hers. I was tempted to do mine really sloppy so she would take my hand as well, but I knew that was cheating; besides, her approval, abstract as it was, was more valuable than her touch at this point.

I glanced over at Mary Beth's page. She was doing very well, a full line ahead of me. I tried to quicken my pace but got sloppy and slowed down for precision's sake. My mechanical pencil was wearing down. I twisted the eraser for more lead. A girl in the middle of the room raised her hand.

Sister glanced quickly at the chart on her desk, then looked up. "Yes, Miss Leonetti."

"My point broke, Sister."

"Go to the pencil sharpener, then, dear."

What luck. Permission to leave your seat and go to the windowsill where the gray steel pencil sharpener stood, with a hole for the pencil on one side, a crank on the other. Inside was a strange and intricate gear mechanism that would magically do the job, filling the belly of the holding can with sweet sawdust and graphite, and leaving the pencil with a point unobtainable with the plastic kind. I knew the other limitation of the mechanical pencil—one less reason to leave your seat.

"When you've finished the page, turn it over, put your pencils down, and fold your hands on the desk." Mary Beth beat me by a mile and sat there gloating as I finished. If I had been doing the task with my left hand, I would have won this race, but I had to learn.

"Wh...

...leave one's seat in service to the class. So fair was she that everyone who wanted to got a turn that morning, though the project was interrupted by recess and a group trip to the lavatory. Before we knew it, it was time for lunch.

Lunchtime lasted from 11:55 to 12:40. Some children lived too far away to walk home and back in time, so they brought their lunches in paper bags and ate in the cafeteria where they could also buy milk or orange drink for a nickel, and a soft pretzel for the same price. Luckily I was a "walker," and so I filed out of the school with the others, in complete silence, and down the sidewalk on Bishop Road to my house. There I gave a full report to my mother and younger sisters while I ate my peanut butter and jelly sandwich. Nancy, a year younger, listened carefully. She would have her chance the following year. I showed her my paper with the cross and circles, and she started her own circles in preparation. Mary, just one, scribbled with a crayon. I demonstrated my Pledge of Allegiance stance and then back to school I ran to put in some quality time on the playground before the 12:40 bell.

An aerial view of the playground after lunch and at recess would have yielded a picture from Breughel, with several hundred children involved in a myriad of games. The girls were skipping rope, the boys playing variations of the game of tag—Freeze Tag, Slow Motion Tag, Stick-on Tag. There were mixed-gender games of kickball, square ball, catch, and keepaway, and all kinds of taunting and chasing. When the bell rang, everyone froze—kickball in mid-kick, jump rope in mid-jump, taunt in mid-chant. Then, five seconds later, another bell relaxed the carefully breathing statues, and we lined up silently and proceeded into school. Each class lined up in a separate spot, the eighth-graders at one end, the first-graders at the other.

These spots were important because this is also where we would line up for a fire drill. That very afternoon we had our first taste of this ritual. As soon as we got back to our classroom, Sister Virginia Mary began to prepare us. Orderly silence was the secret of the fire drill. We were to stand quietly by our desks as soon as we heard the alarm go off, file silently out of the building and take our places in the yard, as we did at recess, until the all-clear signal was sounded, then file back in.

This practice of filing silently is one of the great secrets of Catholic education. Add a few simple elements, and the result is a May procession, the great sign of the Catholic ability to move peacefully in great numbers. The Catholic contribution to the peace movement of the sixties was not a few priests visible at the front of the demonstration but the thousands of lay people with May Procession experience marching behind.

As we stood in lines outside the building for that first fire drill, Sister showed us one of the essential elements by having us line up by size. In the classroom our order was alphabetical, in procession it was genetic. For first-graders the issue was not as painful as it would become in the upper grades, when Mother Nature would begin to separate the short and long of it, as it were, resulting in a kind of cruel exposé of the pubescent tall girls and late-blooming short boys. (Another aspect of lining up by size is the Trinitarian nature of the activity—you need three people to stand in line.)

...Catholic training...well the temper of the times. The Cold War was at its height, McCarthy was on TV after school, people were building bomb shelters in their back yards. Catholic doctrine referred to the faithful on earth as "the Church Militant," whose members, when they were confirmed, were struck on the cheek by the Bishop, sealing them as "soldiers of Christ."

Later on we would hear horror stories about Communist mistreatment of Catholics, and by fifth grade the possibility of being gunned down by a Commie soldier invading our classroom and demanding us to betray our faith—or else—was real in our minds. But this day we only had to learn what to do in case of aerial attack.

"Now, children, an air raid drill is different from a fire drill, because in an air raid we don't go outside. Instead, you get under your desk and cover your head. Now let's try it. Remember, silently, silently. When I count to three, quietly get under your desk and cover your head. One, two, three."

There wasn't exactly enough room for the four of us—Mary Beth, our Guardian Angels, and me—but we made the best of it. The strange silliness of the whole business actually took the edge off the horror we would have felt if we had realized fully what was going on. After we had quieted down in this position, Sister said, "Now all clear, return to your seats." We did so, our hands on our desks, and waited as Sister passed out more paper for the afternoon penmanship lesson. This time it was straight lines, up and down. By the end of the day, we were exhausted, and the lower half of the blackboard was gray from the chalk dust.

"If anyone would like to volunteer to help clean up after school, raise your hand. Walkers only."

Here was my chance to further my training as a Christian Gentleman. My hand shot up at this second chance to shamelessly ingratiate myself with the nuns.

Although cleaning up after school would become a technique of punishment in high school, for me it would be a real pleasure, especially wiping the blackboards. The ones at Holy Cross were genuine slate, none of these green composite things that have signaled the death of real education in the United States. All day long the boards were written upon by teacher and student alike, error and truths cast together. All day long the mistakes would be erased with bricks of felt, leaving a grayish-white film of chalk dust behind, so that there was always visible a hint of past mistakes from past lessons.

But that day I had the pleasure and honor of taking a cotton cloth down to the boys' bathroom, drenching and wringing it, and starting at the upper left-hand corner of the board, standing on a chair in order to reach the top, exorcising the ghosts of past mistakes, until the board was wiped clean, literally. Tabula rasa.

When I learned the next year that my soul was like a milk bottle drawn on the blackboard, with sins chalked in, this wiping clean would take on theological dimensions, suggesting that I was participating in some kind of blackboard absolution of my own sins, but on this first day the experience was simple and grand. I was learning to be a Good Christian Gentleman, helpful, obedient, in service to my first grade nun, always leaving room for my Guardian Angel.

My second-grade classroom at Holy Cross Elementary School was a school bus parked outside the auditorium. The building that housed the rest of the grades was only a year old, but already it was overcrowded. The Baby Boom had hit our community harder than expected, and the educational facilities for Catholic families were especially taxed, for obvious reasons—Catholics had more children, and they tended to "ghettoize" new housing developments, even in the twentieth century. Entire parishes in Southwest Philadelphia moved their grown children and grandchildren into the newly created suburbs of Westbrook Park and Colonial Park that populated Holy Cross Parish.

In some rows in Westbrook Park every family had children in the parochial school. Our row was not one of these. We, in fact, had more "publics"—as we called the children who went, by bus, to the seemingly distant Primos School—than Catholics. Only the Halls, who lived next door with seven kids, and our parents, who would soon have four, sent their progeny to Holy Cross.

There were great debates among the neighborhood kids as to the respective value of the different forms of education. We had uniforms, discipline, Religious Education, nuns—

and we could walk to school; they had bad kids, sloppy clothes, atheism, overpaid lay teachers—and had to ride buses. This last criticism was weakened, however, when I entered second grade and it was clear that though I could walk to school, once I got there I walked into a bus.

One positive aspect of the arrangement, however, was the fact that the number of seats on the bus effectively cut our class size from one hundred eight to forty-four. This was balanced by some negatives, though. For one thing, there was no desk onto which our hands could be folded. Not only did this mean there was greater potential for mischief, but no desk meant no secure writing surface. My handwriting degenerated to a scrawl. In the middle of October we had to keep our overcoats on, slowing down my hand-raising speed. We had no wraparound blackboards to walk up to and show off arithmetic skills on, or to clean after school. Sister Mary Patricia had a small portable blackboard, however, on which we would learn the dynamism of sin on soul in preparation for our first Holy Communion which would take place in the spring of the school year.

For seven years we had watched older children and adults walk reverently in single file up to the altar rail and kneel, then throw their heads back and stick out their tongues to receive a wafer, then return, hands folded in prayer, to their seats, put their heads in their hands and talk directly to Jesus. Being denied this experience for so long made it doubly important. You couldn't just go up and do it, however; you had to be prepared with catechism and practice.

Furthermore, you had to be prepared for a sacrament that preceded reception, which wiped away your sins and made you worthy to receive the Host, as the wafer was called. This was, of course, the Sacrament of Penance, popularly known as Confession.

None of these mysteries could be experienced until a child had reached the Age of Reason, the level of development where you knew wrong from right. Since in Catholic tradition this occurred at age seven, second grade was the logical time for a child's first Communion. A bus was not necessarily the best place to learn about it. Luckily, winter saved us from our modular classroom. In New Mass,

funeral masses each year, since the auditorium was the church as well. We would be in the middle of a flash-card drill when the back door would open and a line of sobbing people would enter the space. The organ would start playing, and our lessons would stop. We were required to watch silently the proceedings or write quietly on our laps. At least we each had our own chair in the auditorium.

The presence of death in our curriculum was well timed, considering the lessons we were learning; as the Apostle says, "The wages of Sin is Death," and dying in the state of Mortal Sin meant eternal damnation of the immortal soul. The distinction between Mortal and Venial Sin is probably what the Age of Reason is all about. And there was a classic motif to help us understand: the milk bottle.

I'm not sure that the motif was used at the Council of Baltimore, which developed the American Catechism in 1888–89, nor do I know what image is used now, when milk bottles have been replaced with cardboard cartons, but in 1953, every second-grader at Holy Cross School had milk delivered in clear glass quart bottles to his or her door by uniformed milkmen. And every second-grader learned the difference between the kinds of sin exemplified by the condition of this handy visual aid. None of us had ever seen a really dirty milk bottle, but we saw many drawings of it that year.

Sister began by walking up to the blackboard with a piece of chalk and saying: "Today we will learn the difference between Mortal Sin and Venial Sin, and Original Sin. First of all, children, who can tell me what a sin is?"

Hands went up, mine among them, "Ssster, Ssster"— this word pronounced without the *i*, in a strained voice, the student almost leaving his seat though never fully, as that would disqualify him from being called on.

"Yes, Edward."

I stood and said in a loud voice: "A sin is a turning away from God who deserves our love."

"Very good, Edward. Now who can tell me what the first sin is called?"

"Ssster, Ssster."

"Yes, Mary Beth."

Mary Beth stood. "The first sin, which we all share, is called Original Sin, it is on our souls when we are born. And it comes from Adam and Eve, who disobeyed God."

"Very good, Mary Beth. Who can tell me what this is?" she asked, drawing something that looked vaguely like an upside-down exclamation mark. Later the representation would degenerate into an amoeboid shape.

"Ssster, Ssster." Not as many hands were up this time. Mine was up from habit. I wasn't sure what I would say if called on, but I was confident in my safety since I'd already had a turn.

"Yes, Daniel?" A big mistake. Dan Carney, who rarely knew the answer, made a sport of guessing by reading the teacher's body language.

"A sin?" he said, to muffled laughter behind hands and up sleeves. Sister tried to cover for him.

"Not exactly, Daniel, we'll see sin in a minute. This is something someone delivers to your house."

"A pizza?" said Dan, trying to recover.

"Ssster."

"Jeannie?"

"A milk bottle?"

"Very good, Jeannie. You can sit down

[text obscured by black mark]

"Yes, sister." There were tears in Kathy's eyes.

Sister began to fill in the bottle, turning the chalk on its side. "This is like Original Sin. When you are born, your soul is like a dirty milk bottle, all covered with Original Sin."

"Ssster, Ssster." My hand shot up. I knew the next answer was Baptism even before the question was asked.

To Sister's surprise, Dan Carney's hand was also up. "Daniel?"

"Limbo?"

Sister was taken aback by this answer. It fit a question several steps away.

"We'll talk about Limbo in a minute, Daniel, sit down."

"Ssster."

"Edward."

"I was going to say how the Original Sin was taken off the soul."

"Very well, how is Original Sin taken off the soul?"

"Ssster, Ssster, Ssster." Dan wanted to regain face. But it was my turn.

"By Baptism?" I said quickly.

"That's right, Baptism takes all the sin away." She erased the chalk from inside the bottle, taking some of the edge with it. She began to redraw it.

"Now what happens if a person dies without any sins at all?"

"Ssster, Ssster."

"Robert?"

"They go directly to Heaven to be with God forever." With my mind's eye, I saw the small white casket covered with flowers from the week before, when a four-year-old polio victim had been the focus of a funeral mass. The priest had worn white instead of the usual black and had spoken of the joys of Heaven, though not vividly enough to persuade the family not to cry their eyes out.

"And what happens to the soul"—she continued, returning to her picture—"when we commit a sin?" She was moving the chalk toward the bottle, telegraphing the correct answer.

"Ssster."

"Yes, Elizabeth?"

"We get a mark on it?"

"Right, Elizabeth," she said, making marks as she spoke. "Each time we disobey our parents, a mark, each time we disobey our teachers, a mark, each time we don't do our homework, a mark, each time we disobey a commandment or precept of the Church, a mark, each time we cheat, a mark."

All of our faces were reddening to some degree; we had truly reached the Age of Reason. The bottle was filling up, with only a few spaces left.

"These sins with little marks are called Venial Sins," she continued. "Say that."

"Venial Sins," we chanted.

"Now there is a kind of sin that is more serious than Venial, like murder or adultery, and this kind of sin is called

Mortal Sin, and it covers the whole milk bot— I mean the whole soul." Again she turned the chalk on its side, keeping in the lines as well as she could. "And if you die with Mortal sin on your soul, you go to…"

"Ssster, Ssster."

"Maria?"

an eternity." She went on with the lesson. "Now here's the big question…"

"Ssster, Ssster."

"Yes, Daniel?"

"Baptism?"

"Wait for my question, Daniel. How do we cleanse our soul from both Mortal and Venial—but not necessarily Original—sin?"

"Ssster, Ssster." An easy question.

"Mike?"

"The Sacrament of Penance. By going to Confession."

"Very good, Mike."

"Ssster." Patricia Ronan's hand was up. When called on she asked, "Where do babies go that aren't baptized but don't have any sins of their own?"

"*Sssssster, Sssssster.*" Dan Carney was straining so hard on this one I was sure he was going to wet his pants, as he had on Hallowe'en listening to a scary story.

"Daniel."

Dan stood triumphantly, looking around to make sure we were listening to his act of self-justification. "Limbo, like

I said before. Unbaptized babies go to Limbo, unless they committed a sin."

"Like what?" All eyes were on Jackie Woulfe. "What sin could a baby commit?"

Dan's face reddened. He had been doing so well.

"Jack Woulfe, did you raise your hand?" Sister was doing her best to protect Dan from the class renegade, using parliamentary procedure to soften the blow.

"No, Sister, I'm sorry." He raised his hand, reluctantly.

"Yes?"

"I just thought that you had to be in second grade before you could commit a sin." I was beginning to suspect that my friend Jackie had reached the Age of Reason before he entered school.

"That's right, Jack, but raise your hand from now on."

A hand went up.

"Yes, Constance?"

"Sister, what about pagans, who never heard about Baptism, what about pagan adults in some undiscovered island?"

This was the opening volley of a game of Doctrinal Tennis that we Catholic kids would play with our Religion teachers as long as we went to Catholic school. There was much in the tradition that was debatable, we would find, though there was something at the base of it all which was not. Testing our teachers on points of logic would become a sport for some of us, pushing them as hard as we could until they broke down and ended the negotiations or fell back on the authority of the Church by claiming that the issue under discussion was a "mystery." Sister's face was gaining color in anticipation of what might come.

"That is a very good question, Constance," said Sister, trying to gain time to answer. "As you know, we try to ransom pagan babies and baptize them whenever we can. That's why we send money to the Missions. But if a person is not baptized because he never heard of it, then that person, if he leads a good life with the use of his reason, will not go to Hell, he will go to Limbo."

Some fun that would be, I thought, a good pagan adult or two and millions of screaming ~~babies. No Hell~~

~~a disputed question.~~

"Now we don't know for sure who is in Heaven or who is in Hell, or Limbo, or Purgatory. But we do know that God judges each person on what is in their heart, and we know that the Seven Maccabbees, who were Jewish, are in Heaven because of Baptism of Blood. You'll learn next year that there are three types of baptism: Baptism of Water, Baptism of Desire, and Baptism of Blood."

She was getting off the hook, thank goodness, by talking over our heads. I was relieved, feeling like a traitor for bringing up the question.

"So there might be Jews in Heaven from Baptism of Blood and Baptism of Desire?" I asked, trying to realign myself as her ally.

"We won't know until we get there," she said, calming down and smiling. Over the next dozen years, this answer would end several such debates, making the solution of all sorts of questions a prime reason to try to get to Heaven, where we would find out what Jesus looked like, what kind of wings angels had, whether Adam and Eve had belly buttons, and what was in the Letter from Fatima about the end of the world that the Pope had read and cried over.

Sister looked a little weary. She reached under the large starched bib that covered her front almost from neck to diaphragm and retrieved the small watch she kept there. Relieved at what she saw on its face, she smiled sweetly.

"Recess, children, line up. Tomorrow be sure you know the three signs of Mortal Sin, and the first two lines of the Act of Contrition. Tomorrow we will practice going to Confession."

This last announcement struck terror in my heart for two reasons. First, there was a residual fear of the dark that made going into the confessional booth a little scary, but worse than this was an ethical problem—coming up with some good sin without lying in the act of Penance, which was itself a great sin. After all, I was a good boy, always had been. I had won the General Excellence Medal the year before, I'd been carrying Sister's bag and staying after school to help clean, I did my homework every night, I ate all my vegetables. How I envied Joe Quinn. He was a bad boy. A kid like him would have no problem. There must be something I could confess. Tomorrow would be easy. It wasn't real—Sister would play the part of the priest—so I could make up some sins without committing a sin by reporting them.

But I only had three weeks to come up with some real sins. Maybe I could commit a sin just for the occasion. But what if I died before I got to Confession? Maybe I could commit a sin the day or, even better, the night before. But I could still die in my sleep. The thing to do would be to commit a sin right before confession time. What were my chances of that? I was in a quandary.

Things didn't get any better that night as I memorized the three conditions for a Mortal Sin. They were "Grievous Matter, Sufficient Reflection, and Full Consent of the Will." I had passed the Age of Reason, but the vocabulary here was beyond my understanding. I was pretty sure I knew what Full Consent of the Will was: you really want to do a thing,

and no one is forcing you. Later on, when concupiscence—
that effect of Original Sin which makes us prone to sin—really kicked in, this third requirement would be the loophole
of a fantasy I enjoyed where I was kidnapped by four
beautiful girls in a car...

...Mortal Sin are you working on?"

I missed the joke. "Mortal."

"Oh, big time, and what particular Mortal Sin are you
working on tonight?"

"All of them."

"All at once? You're not John Dillinger, are you?"

"No," I laughed, finally getting his joke. "I'm working
on the definition of Mortal Sin, not any particular one."

"Whew, I thought for a second there I had a real bad
character under the roof. Want me to hear your catechism?"

"That would be great. We only have one question, and
the beginning of the Act of Contrition."

"Sounds good. Let me hear the prayer first."

My father was a Protestant, but this didn't keep him
from helping with Religion homework. He had, after all, had
to promise the priest that he would raise his kids in the Faith
before he was allowed to marry my mother. Theirs was a
"mixed marriage," a kind which the catechism would warn
about.

I began the prayer. "'O My God, I am heartily sorry for
having offended Thee, and I detest all my sins, because I
dread the loss of Heaven and the pains of Hell.' That's all we
need to know so far."

"Very good. Now, the catechism question. What are the three requirements for a sin to be mortal?"

"The three requirements for a sin to be mortal"—the catechism answers always repeated the question—"are Grievious Matter, Sufficient Reflection, and Full Consent of the Will."

"*Grievous* Matter, not grievious."

"But Sister and everybody in the class say 'grievious.'"

"If Sister and everybody in the class jumped off a cliff, would you do it too?"

This was the first time I had heard that classic argument. It conjured a vision in my mind of forty-three children and a black-veiled nun sailing out into thin air as in a "Road Runner" cartoon, and me standing along at the edge of a cliff, friendless, but right.

"No, but..." A voice way in the back of my head was whispering, *What do you know, you're Protestant.* I stuttered and kept quiet. I began again. "Grievous Matter, Sufficient Reflection, and Full Consent of the Will."

"That's my boy. Is there anything else you need help with?"

"No, that's all we had. Thanks, Dad."

I was glad to end the moment. I didn't like disagreeing with him. I went upstairs and got ready for bed, the germ of a solution to my problem of Sin beginning to grow in my mind.

The next day, Sister Mary Patricia brought some friends with her—two aged nuns who had come to help with the confession practice. One of them would monitor the class while the other one would man the confessionals with Sister Mary Patricia.

Since our classroom was the church auditorium, we did not have to go elsewhere for this exercise. Built into the back wall of the large room were two sets of three doors. The center door of each of these sets had a cross that lit up if a priest, or anyone posing as a priest, occupied the chair in the closet behind the door. On either side of the chair were two small windows with opaque plastic screens through which the penitent, kneeling in

could be heard, and sometimes the clear voice of the priest asking questions of the other penitent. Then the mumbling would stop and the door would slide back, revealing the profile of the priest, and the confession would begin.

Outside the confessional other penitents would wait in line, not close enough to hear the proceedings but ready to occupy a booth as soon as it became empty. Later on in my career as a sinner, I would learn the pressure that waiting classmates could apply to a person in terms of time spent. If a confession went longer than average, it was a sign of having sinned too much. When we were in second grade, though, this nuance was lost on us.

"This is Sister Mary Consuela from the Mother House," Sister said. An ancient nun smiled at us.

We all stood and bowed or curtseyed. "Good morning, Sister Mary Consuela."

"And this is Sister Mary Edward from the Hospital." This one was big, with a stern face. She would be the monitor.

"Good morning, Sister Mary Edward." We all bowed or curtseyed again, then sat down.

"Now class, today we're going to practice going to Confession. You don't have to worry about what sins you are going to confess. Just make it up—you can wait until

Father is here before you confess your real sins. Now the first row line up outside of the confessionals on the right, half on each side, and the second row line up at the ones on the left. That's it. Sister Mary Edward will be watching you, so cross your lips, and be quiet."

We all put the sign of the cross on our lips, thus making any conversation a breach of a religious oath. Since I was in the third row, I would have to wait. I went over the opening words in my mind. *Bless me Father, for I have sinned, this is my first Confession.* Then I opened my catechism to the Examination of Conscience in the back. This was a list of questions for reflection in preparation for Confession. It took each of the Commandments and Precepts of the Church in turn, and asked questions about possible sins. I combed through the questions, looking for a good one to use. Murder looked like my best bet. I'd use that today, but what would I do in three weeks, when a real priest would be sitting on the other side of the screen?

Then it hit me. I could lie to the priest at my first Confession and then get back in line to confess that I had lied in Confession. I wondered how possible this plan was. Tommy O'Leary had just come out of the confessional on the right and was proceeding to the front to kneel at the altar rail to say his penance. Would it be possible to return to line instead of to the seat? I looked around and saw Sister Mary Edward scanning the room with the eyes of a hawk. Not a chance.

Besides, lying in Confession was probably a Mortal Sin. I went over the categories. Would I have Full Consent of the Will? Yes, no one was forcing me to do it, unless the whole system of Religion Class was, but that was too abstract to think about until high school. No, I would have full consent in this case.

What about Sufficient Reflection? Well, I was reflecting sufficiently right now; three more weeks and the reflection would be quite sufficient. How about Grievious Matter. Lying in Confession would certainly be grievous. My soul would be condemned to Hell, but only, if the plan worked, for a very short time—the time it would take to sneak back in line. Sneak back in line

g— go to Hell if I died before the following Saturday.

It was too great a risk. If only lying in Confession were not so grievous. I mean grievous. Eureka, I had it. A Venial Sin for sure, but a concrete one—I could disobey my father by pronouncing a word the way he told me not to. The word was *grievious*, but the matter wasn't grievous, plus there wouldn't be *full* consent of the will, because Sister pronounced it that way, and the teacher is always right, and in disobeying my father, I was obeying her, jumping off a cliff for just a moment. The Age of Reason was kind of fun.

My row's turn finally came, and we lined up. All I had to do was pronounce a word wrong, and I'd be a sinner, not just a pretend murderer. Mary Watson came out of the closet and held the door for me. I entered and closed the door behind me, knelt down on the wooden kneeler and tried to hear Sister Mary Consuela. She was speaking too low. Suddenly the door slid back, and I began.

"Bless me Father, for I have sinned, this is my first Confession and I have committed a sin of grievious matter. I killed a man in cold blood."

There, I had disobeyed my father. I had a real sin to confess.

"How many times?" came the frail voice of a nun who was trying her best to be a good priest. How many times had I disobeyed my father, or murdered a man in cold blood? Could she hear my words, or was she deaf and had ESP? Luckily the answer was the same.

"One."

"Anything else?"

"No, nothing else."

"Are you sorry for your sin?"

Which one, the imagined murder, or lying to my father? If the latter, I might get forgiven now for the sin I needed to keep until my real Confession. If the former, I would be lying to say I felt sorry for a sin I did not commit. Is lying to a nun in pretend Confession worse than disobeying your father? Is it a sin at all?

"No," I whispered. *I hope you're deaf,* I thought silently.

She was.

"Very good, say three Hail Marys and sin no more. Now say the Act of Contrition."

I said what I knew of the Act of Contrition and walked out, holding the door for Jackie Woulfe. I walked up to the front and knelt down. I said the prayers. As I was walking back to my seat a horrible thought hit me. Was hoping a nun was deaf a sin? I ran down the three requirements for Mortal Sin and was relieved to figure out that it was not Grievous Matter. It probably was a Venial Sin, though, giving me two sins to confess three weeks later.

By the time I went to my first real Confession, I had developed a repertoire of venials and was well on my way to developing what is known as a "Scrupulous Conscience." I would become, in popular Catholic parlance, a "Scrupe." This kind of thinking would serve me well years later on my college boards.

Second grade was a busy year for us at Holy Cross, sacramentally speaking. Shortly after our first Penance came our first Holy Communion. The preparation for this event was not as complex as it had been for Penance. There was no interaction to rehearse, and the only activity we had to learn was throwing our heads back and sticking out our tongues as we knelt at the altar rail. The theology, however, was no less interesting.

For weeks we had been memorizing the answers to catechism questions concerning the Doctrine of Transubstantiation whereby Christ's Real Presence is made tangible in the Sacrament of the Lord's Supper.

"Now, children, what happens to the Bread and Wine on the altar when the priest performs the Consecration?" Sister asked.

"The Bread and Wine are turned into the Body and Blood of Christ," we sang out in unison.

"Do the Bread and Wine change in appearance?"

"The Bread and Wine do not change in appearance, but only in substance."

This distinction between substance and appearance (or "accident," as it was known in the catechism) was based on

medieval rules of Philosophy that we would never com-
prehend. Luckily there were stories to help us understand
the great mystery.

My favorite was the story of the bad boy who took the
Host out of his mouth after receiving it and put it in his
pocket until he got home. He locked himself in his room and
then, to prove to himself that it was "just bread," nailed it to
his wall. Blood came pouring out of the wounded wafer and
the boy drowned in it, presumably going to Hell for eternity.
Some Protestant part of me figured that the lesson was about
not locking the door of your room when you tried such
shenanigans, but the rest of me was cowed with reverence.

Although we had not yet received the Bread in our
mouths, we knew how special the sacrament was from
watching others return from the altar rail in an attitude of
hushed contemplation. We had also been present at Benedic-
tion, when the priest, his hands in a special cloth called a
cope, raised a special reliquary with one large wafer in a glass
window in the middle of gold filigree, and blessed the community with it. And we had been present for Forty Hours
Devotion, when this reliquary, called the monstrance, was
placed alone on the altar for the length of time our Lord spent
in the tomb. At Forty Hours there was only silent meditation
and contemplation, and genuflection on two knees, instead
of the customary one.

Preparation for first Holy Communion also included
getting a new outfit, which we would also wear in the May
Procession that year. For the boys, it was composed of white
shoes, white socks, white pants, white shirt, white jacket, and
white tie. The white was meant to show our purity, as we
had recently received our first Confession. The event would
be followed by a reception at our house, where I would
receive presents.

The day finally came, and I reported in white to the
church, taking my place with my classmates. Everybody

looked wonderful, scrubbed and rosy. The girls were dressed in beautiful white dresses, the Italians a little grander that the Irish, more lace and crinoline. We had been practicing for weeks, learning to process, genuflect, and all the rest. We used Necco wafers in our rehear...

...pressing a Freihofer's slice between heavy volumes of the *History of Napoleon*, my father's prize possession, but I was never to get the thinness or stiffness of the Holy Bread, which I now know was made by cloistered Franciscan nuns.

When the time finally came to receive, we filed out to the middle aisle and up to the altar rail. I knelt and waited. The back of my neck was burning from the eyes of all the parents staring at us. I was nervous, afraid the Host might pop out of my mouth as an omen of my unworthiness and embarrass me and my entire family.

The priest was two people down, and coming fast. I tried to think if there were any sins on my soul since Confession, and said an Act of Contrition just in case. My soul was as clean a milk bottle as it would ever be. The altar boy accompanying the priest stepped backwards and placed a golden plate under my chin—in case the Host did pop out—and the priest lifted a host out of the ciborium and held it before my eyes. I closed them, tossed my head back as far as I could, opened my mouth as wide as it would go and, getting my cues confused, said, "Aaah." I felt the plate hit my Adam's apple and opened my eyes to see the altar boy trying not to laugh. Father's face was red, but not from anger.

"It's OK, son, open up one more time."

I did so, and felt the wafer light on the tip of my tongue. I pulled it in and closed my mouth. Finally I had Jesus inside of me. I rose from the altar rail, turned around and started back to my seat, my hands folded in reverence. I began to talk to Jesus.

My lips were closed, but my jaw still hung down in order not to insult Jesus by chewing Him with my teeth. As I silently thanked him for all the good things in my life, I tried to manipulate the Host with my tongue toward my throat. I succeeded only in plastering the wafer to the roof of my mouth, where it stuck. I tried to work it loose, but to no avail. When I tried to suck it down, odd noises began to issue from within, like the sound of an open-face peanut butter sandwich without the jelly.

Instinctively, my hand went toward my mouth, index finger poised (like the peanut butter joke my Aunt Bet would sometimes do) but then the picture of the boy drowning in blood flooded my brain, and I stopped. If I touched the Host I would be doomed to Hell. If I let it stay there, I would never to able to eat—the Host must not touch normal food. My classmates and I had been fasting since midnight the day before.

I would starve to death. But what a glorious way to go. Surely I would go directly to Heaven if I died in such a way. A mental picture of Jesus welcoming a boy in his Holy Communion togs to Heaven replaced the image of the bad boy, and I felt somewhat calmer, my tongue still searching for a way under the wafer, which was now beginning to dissolve somewhat, small pieces sliding down my throat.

The organist started playing "Salve Regina." It was time to rise and sing, which I did without opening my mouth. As we processed out, there were still particles pressed into the masonry of the roof of my mouth, which only water could loosen, I hoped.

At the door of the church, my family was waiting to congratulate me. I grunted my responses, trying not to be impolite, and smiled without opening my mouth, my tongue still hard at work. When we all started back to the house, I ran ahead, dashed upstairs, and

...learning that it's sometimes best to keep your mouth shut, and I knew that appearances were sometimes very tricky.

...chanical or handy with tools ...ing things. The basements of the row houses of Westbrook Park were not large enough for a very big workshop with saws and drills, although Mr. Forbes next door had a fine version of a workshop, with jars of nails of different sizes hung by their lids overhead. It was like a small hardware store in itself. He also had a small worktable flush against the wall with a vise, some handsaws hanging above it, all manner of screwdrivers, hammers, an axe, and even a small power saw.

Mr. Forbes was what you might call "handy." My father, I guess, was "footy" in comparison—he was a great dancer but not good with tools.

The first Christmas after I had reached the Age of Reason (in the Catholic tradition, this was the age of seven, after which one could be held "culpable" for one's actions), my father built something that would be the center of Christmases all through my youth.

In our Westbrook Park row house, the lower level opened only out the back of the house. It was divided into two spaces, the cellar and the garage. The garage was just large enough to house the Plymouth Cedarbrook and very little else, so that when my Dad started parking in front of the house after work, my sister Nancy—even though she had not passed the Age of Reason yet—and I knew something was going on in the garage. After dinner, he would loudly announce, "I'm going to take the garbage down, Anne," and disappear down the steps to the basement and out the back door. We would hear the door close behind him, the garbage pail open, receive its gift, then be gonged shut.

After that, instead of the basement door reopening, there would be a pause, followed by the sound of a lock tumbler releasing; then the sound of the garage door, which was on poorly greased tracks, being lifted inch by inch, as close to silently as he could manage it, which was absurd then and now comical and dear, since, when opened normally, the door shook the whole house.

As my sister helped my mother clear the table, I would nonchalantly go over to the window and look out on the back lawn, lit by the hundred-watt exposed bulb in the garage, trying to see from the shadows what my father was doing. If my mother caught me looking, she would draft me into helping in the kitchen.

One night during this time, I sneaked downstairs to listen through the cellar wall. I heard sawing followed by the marimbic sound of pieces of two-by-four boards hitting the concrete floor, then hammering interspersed with angry responses to thumb pain. I began to distinguish the sounds of metal on board from metal on flesh on board, cued as the latter were by the angry grunts, never curses. My father never cursed. After a particularly loud metal-flesh-board strike, I heard the back door open. Hiding behind an old wardrobe, I listened as my father came through the basement and disappeared up the stairs.

"Do we have any Bandaids, hon?"

"Upstairs in the medicine chest, Alvey."

Now was my chance. I tiptoed quickly to the door, and out. Standing at the entrance to the garage, I caught a glimpse of the top-secret project: a large piece of plywood braced on one side with two-by-fours, and painted green on the other side. I tiptoed back [illegible] face in disgust, "That's all?"

"That's all I could see."

She went back to her homework, making circles like a Slinky between two lines. She was in first grade. I took my homework out of my bookbag. A brown-paper-covered catechism and a marble-covered notebook would be my focus for the next half hour. I opened the book to the questions on the Holy Eucharist. I took a pencil out of my pencil case and found that it was dull, the point too thick to yield well-defined letters on the page. I got up from the dinner table and walked over to the table by the window which held the telephone, desserts on Sunday, and the pencil sharpener, screwed to the corner. This pencil sharpener was the reason, I think, for any success I had in grade school. It was exactly like the ones at school—detachable metal cover which held the sawdust and lead dust, real metal gears inside and a metal handle which you turned until the point was sharp. Most of the other kids at school had those plastic ones with a single blade into which you inserted the pencil and twirled the pencil against the blade. Even today I cannot get a real pencil point with these ill-conceived contraptions. Having a real pencil sharpener in our home was a sign of how much my father valued our education.

Pencil sharpened, I sat down again across from Nancy, who was still doodling. She looked up.

"Ping-pong?" she queried, a little skeptically. Our cousins in Jersey had ping-pong, but it wasn't our favorite game. Besides, where would we put it? Neither of us had asked Santa Claus for it. Nancy had asked for Barbie and I had asked for badminton and books. But ping-pong?

I set to my work, writing out the questions and answers from the catechism. Only five had to be done, and they were mostly short. Nancy finished her Slinkys and closed her book, putting it in her bag.

"Where would we put a ping-pong table?" she asked.

"I don't know," I said. "Can't put it downstairs, no room."

"Unless they move the cedar chest and wardrobe into the garage."

"Then there won't be any room for the car."

"The living room's the only place," I said.

"But then where will we put the furniture so we won't trip over it when we play?"

"I don't know. Shhh, here he comes," I whispered, my head buried in the notebook, at the sounds of my father coming up the steps. We had not even heard the garage door being closed, so intense was our inquiry. He came through the door into the dining room. His bandaged thumb showed red.

"Everybody done their homework?"

"I am, I am, wanna see?" said Nancy proudly, producing her notebook, open to the circles.

"Learning to write, I see, very nice. You keep between the lines real well. Your handwriting will take after your mother's, I think, neat and fine, not like mine." He hadn't gone to parochial school. "Eddie, what about you?"

"Almost finished, Dad, just Catechism—written." I wanted to make it clear that these particular questions were

not to be memorized yet, that I wouldn't need him to help
by asking me the questions. That was always hard on both
of us, me wanting to get the answers letter-perfect, him not
always understanding the answers or the questions, since he
was Protestant, both of us feelin

"Oh, I hit it with a hammer fixing something in the
garage."

Something like a ping-pong table, I thought to myself,
but said, stupidly, "Does it hurt?"

"Not as much as when you got hit in the head with the
hardball last summer."

"That didn't hurt," I blurted, more to my sister than to
him.

"Then this doesn't either."

I knew from that response that it hurt awfully. But he
was a guy. And so was I.

After the injury, he laid off the project in the garage for
a week, and we began to suspect that it wasn't really a
Christmas surprise after all. A week before the big day,
however, he was at it again, and we knew whatever it was
was going under the tree—if it would fit, that is.

The Saturday before Christmas brought disappointing news
in the mail: the photos of me and my sisters with Santa, taken
at Wanamaker's department store in November, had not
turned out. These photos were a great treasure in the family;
we had one from every year since we were tiny. To remedy
the situation, we would have the odd privilege of sitting on

Santa's lap twice this year. So we were bundled up right after lunch and driven downtown for our encore.

It was a treat to visit Wanamaker's any time of the year, but especially at Christmas. Built around the turn of the century, it had the grandeur of a fine hotel. The center court was six stories high, with a balcony around three sides of each floor overlooking the first, the fourth side holding a great wall of bulbs and fountains on which the story of Christmas was told in sound and light.

We arrived in time for the one-thirty show, so we elbowed our way to a position where we could see the spectacle, Nancy and I holding hands, my two-year-old sister, Mary, in my mother's arms. When the lights in the court dimmed and the organ began, my father lifted us up to stand on the gloves case, from which we had a clear view. First an invisible speaker told the story of Rudolph the Red-Nosed Reindeer, as lights depicting the reindeer and Santa flashed, moving magically across the wall as the story ended happily, with Rudolph at the front. Then "The March of the Toy Soldiers" was enacted, arms and legs moving in rhythm. Christmas trees, jacks-in-the-box, ballerinas, bouncing balls, and dolls made of light joined in the finale as the dancing colored fountains of lighted water added a dimension of beauty and danger. Finally the voice of John Facenda, Philadelphia's most famous newscaster, invited us to join in a final rendition of "Jingle Bells." Then it was over, and the crowd began to disperse.

"Come on, kids, let's go upstairs and see Santa," said my father, somewhat edgily. I began to suspect he wasn't having much fun and would rather be at home in the garage.

"Can we take the escalator, Dad?" I asked, knowing the answer before he spoke. The escalator at Wanamaker's was probably the oldest in the world, I always thought. It was very wide and made of wood, and just dangerous enough to be an adventure. The timing of placing your foot on a moving stair so that you weren't hanging off when it gained height after a few feet was something I had not perfected yet. I was jealous of Nancy, who had it down pat, partially, I always felt, from her experience jumping rope and playing hopscotch with her friends.

Nancy was first. She stood there, her hand lightly on one of the moving handrails, counting the cracks in the conveyance that became stairs in seconds. "One, two, three," she stepped confidently out and brought her other foot squarely on a moving step, turned around and smiled teasingly. "Step on a crack, break your back."

I took her place at the top. A line of strangers was beginning to form behind me. The steps were moving fast, the cracks even faster. I started counting "one, two, three," then balked, not confident I could step squarely, my hand grabbing and loosening in turn the moving rubber. My sister, fading into the distance, was still smiling. "Last one down's a monkey's uncle," she taunted. My father passed me on the left with my little sister in his arms and started walking down to catch up with Nancy. My mother gently took my hand and said, "Now," as she stepped on. I pulled my hand away, and said, "No," and watched her descend five steps or so behind my father. I stepped aside to let the strangers go ahead and lost sight of my mother, but heard her voice: "We'll be waiting at the bottom of the escalator. Don't be afraid."

I wasn't afraid, actually, just frustrated that I didn't know a secret that everyone else, including my younger sister, knew. I felt the patronizing stare of the strangers who looked back to see a boy who had reached the Age of Reason but couldn't figure out a simple conveyance: how cute, how sad.

"One, two, three." I counted the cracks and finally stepped out, my right foot squarely on a crack, my left foot apparently on the crack behind, because the heels of both feet were on something solid, albeit at two different heights, and moving forward and apart at the same time, the soles stepping on thin air like a cartoon character off a cliff. I grabbed the moving handrail with both hands and instinctively swung my feet up on it, so that my entire body was being moved by the handrail, my rear end in the air. Suddenly I heard laughter and applause from below. The strangers who passed me were watching from the eighth floor. I looked down at the steps and noticed that they seemed to not be moving, they were going at the same rate as the handrail on which I was riding. I jumped down onto a step and resumed a normal position, assuming an air of nonchalance as though nothing had happened, as the final step-off approached.

Stepping off an escalator is less problematic because the stairs are moving you forward and then disappearing under the metal-toothed comb at the bottom. It's more automatic, but scary nonetheless. But I was not to be pitied. I did not look down when the handrail began to bend, I simply started walking, right into my mother's arms.

"Let me down," I demanded. "I'm not a baby."

She put me down, and we proceeded to Santa's Workshop, actually a maze of barriers and theater-lobby velvet ropes that held the line to Santa. Behind glass cases beside the lines were moving puppets, powered by barely visible pulleys and gears—elves making toys, Victorian children playing with puppies beneath Christmas trees, train sets going through networks of tunnels and mountains. My train set was a wooden job on wooden ruts, powered by hand. I only set it up at the holiday. But these trains were real electric with switches and cars that held real stuff, and there were houses and stations, and even streetlights that lit, and little people, one of whom moved with a lantern when a train came by. Bobby Forbes had such a train set. Electric, on a platform elevated by sawhorses.

The lin~

~y, I'd rather have badminton. You do it."

"I don't want a ping-pong table. You do it."

Mary was really fussing by this time. "Put her down here with us, Mom," Nancy said. "We'll play with her." As soon as she hit the floor, Mary was off and running, going under the barricades that separated the lines heading for the toy department.

"Teddy bears teddy bears," she squealed as she ran. Nancy caught up to her first. I was close behind, as our parents held our place in line. Nancy tried to persuade her to return to the line. When it became clear Mary was not interested, Nancy tried another tactic.

"Look, Mary, Santa Claus's nose." Nancy was trying to draw her attention to the electric pin she wore on her coat, the face of Santa with a nose that lit up when a string beneath the pin was pulled. "Do you want to pull the string?"

"Yes, pull string," Mary replied. As Nancy held the pin so her coat would not be ripped, Mary pulled the string, then squealed with delight. She did it several times. Just as she was getting bored, Nancy decided to pull her into our dilemma.

"What are you going to ask Santa for this year?"

"Baby doll," came the reply.

"What else?"

"Teddy bear."

"Wouldn't you like a ping-pong set?"

"Ping-pong," came the obedient response.

"When you get up to Santa Claus tell him you want ping-pong, OK?"

"Baby doll, teddy bear, pong."

"Ping-pong," I coached. "Ping-pong."

"Pee pong."

"Close enough. Now let's get back in line."

We didn't have long to wait before it was our turn. Santa's helper, an overly made-up girl, from the display department most likely, led the three of us up to Santa, our parents waiting within earshot. As soon as Mary was placed on Santa's lap, she began to cry. Nancy sidled up next to her, and I sat on the other lap, both of us trying to soothe Mary.

"Now what do you want for Christmas, children?" came the traditional question from behind the traditional beard. It was clear that the beard was not connected to the face, but never having seen a Santa with *real* whiskers, I had decided the year before that Santa preferred to wear a fake beard for some reason. Perhaps he was in seasonal disguise, like Superman.

Mary had quieted and was looking up in great fear at the face.

"Tell Santa," urged Nancy. "I want a baby doll."

"Ba' doll," she said in a little voice.

"And how about you, big sister, what do you want?"

"I want a Barbie, and crayons and a pencil box, but she wants something else, too."

"What a good big sister, looking after the little one. What else does she want?"

"Tell Santa. Teddy bear."

"Tehy bear."

"Very good, and young man, what do you want?"

"I want a badminton set with real feathers on the shuttlecock, and books, any kind of books for boys, but Mary wants something else."

Santa looked back at Mary, who had calmed down by now. Nancy was whispering in her ear.

... ping pong, but first a Barbie for me."

"And badminton for me, real badminton, with the feathers."

I looked at my parents, hoping they were pleased with our responses. Apparently, though, they hadn't even heard them.

"Now look at Santa's helper," the girl with the makeup was saying condescendingly. "Smile."

There was a blinding flash of light. Santa gave each of us a candy cane as we slipped off his lap. We ran to our mother as our father gave our address and some money to the girl.

When he joined us again, he said, "Ready for the escalator?"

My heart stopped. I turned and said with false bravado, "All nine floors?"

"If you want," he replied. "But no riding the handrail this time."

"Come on," said Nancy, "I'll show you a trick."

We walked over to the escalator and waited until only a few people stood in line at the top. Nancy took my hand. We stood watching the stainless steel comb release the cracks between the wooden stairs.

"It's just like jump-rope."

"I know that," I said defensively, "but I'm a boy. I don't jump rope."

"Well, the trick is, you step out as soon as the rope goes by. Same thing with the crack. Count with me, on three."

"One," passed the first crack. My heart was pounding, I pulled my hand away. My sister was rocking on the balls of her feet—it *was* just like jump-rope. "Two." The second crack passed. "Three." I placed one foot right behind the crack and the other foot next to it, and found myself moving smoothly down the conveyance, my sister next to me.

"Pretty easy, huh?" she said.

"When you know the trick."

By the fifth floor, I had the knack of it pretty well, and by the third floor I was putting my foot on the crack and riding on my heels, my soles in space before me. (Later on, I would learn to do this right onto the metal teeth at the bottom.)

When we got to the ground floor, we were just in time to sing "Jingle Bells" with the dancing fountains again. Then we were out onto the street, to which Santa Claus had beaten us and where he now stood ringing a bell. I knew it was him by the false beard.

On the way home we stopped to get a tree in a vacant lot near the baseball field. The trees we normally got were always just a tad too tall for our living room, so there was always a trace of resin stain on the ceiling left by the tree at its raising, before the top branch was cut to make room for the angel. Choosing a tree was a chore for my mother, a pleasure for my dad. I loved being out in public with him, watching him charm everyone he met, however briefly.

The girls stayed in the car, Mary alternating between whining and sleeping, Nancy with her arm around her in the back seat, my mother in the front seat going over a list of ingredients for the baked goods she would start making that night.

As Dad and I approached the stand, I asked him what kind of tree we would be getting.

"Balsam fir, son, the kind we alway̲s̲

"Balsam fir smells the sweetest and it doesn't take up all the room like a Scotch pine. Our living room isn't that big you know."

"Big enough for presents, though." I was trying to figure out where the ping-pong table would be on Christmas morning. Each child had a spot on the floor where his presents were placed, to avoid confusion. My presents were always against the wall next to the kitchen, near the entrance to the dining room, Nancy's would be against the perpendicular wall, next to the tree, and Mary's would be against the wall under the stairs, next to the stockings hung from the banisters. My parents left their presents for each other on the love seat against the front wall. Where the ping-pong table would go was a mystery. Since it was a "family present" it should go in the middle of the room, but then you wouldn't be able to come through into the dining room. The only way I could figure doing it was like the Forbes' train set, with the tree on the table. Thus we would need a shorter tree, maybe even a bushy Scotch pine. A shorter balsam fir, as sweet as it might smell, would be a joke, even mounted on a ping-pong table.

But it was not a shorter tree Alvey Stivender was looking for. My theory was dashed when he said to the shivering attendant, a college kid, "Where's your nine-footers?"

"We have some nine-foot trees over here, I don't think we have any pines that big." He led us down a needle-strewn aisle between hastily built corrals of trees with different colored ribbons. Some of the trees were bound with sisal twine. The smell was intoxicating. I had had only seven Christmases up to that point, but I knew the smell. We came to a corral with a handmade sign: FIRS—$12. There were about six trees propped up against the corral boards, some still bound.

My father chose what looked like the bushiest, and held it up straight. It extended about a yard above his head. Then he looked at me and said, "Watch if any needles fall." He lifted the tree and brought the trunk down hard against the ground, twice. A few needles fell with a subtle tinkling sound.

"Are they green or brown?"

I hadn't noticed. He did it again. A few more needles fell, all brown.

"All brown, sir," I reported.

He winked at me, then said to the kid, "Bad sign, brown needles. This tree's already dead, won't last the night." He paused.

The kid was frowning. "Nobody's complained before about this batch."

"How many gave it the brown needle test?"

"Well, no one, but..."

"Is the manager around?"

"Nawh, my dad's gone home for his dinner break, he'll be back in a half hour."

The mention of dinner made me hungry. Since this was Saturday, we'd have steak and potatoes, green beans, and Hanscom's cinnamon nut cake for dessert. The sun had gone down—it was only four-thirty—the sky was the color of watermelon rind, and I began to feel cold. Inside me a voice not unlike my little sisters' began to whine. My teeth began to chatter. I silenced the voice with a silent Hail Mary, and watched my dad.

"You know you're right." They both laughed, the boy wasn't frowning any more. "I'll tell you what, I'll give you eight dollars for this scrawny tree and a dollar tip for your education fund."

At the mention of the bargain price, the kid's jaw hardened, but the education fund idea seemed to seal the deal. When we got back to the car, both sisters were asleep. It was my mother's turn to be edgy.

"I thought you two had bought out the business. What took you so long?"

"Establishing rapport, my dear, establishing rapport, the first task of a good entrepreneur." I wasn't sure until years later exactly what these words meant, but I suspected it had to do with asking the kid about school, and softening him up with the tip. "Nothing like a satisfied customer."

"Or a satisfied salesman," I piped in.

"Right you are, my lad, right you are. Eddie, stand on the other side of the car and catch this rope."

He had hoisted the tree onto the roof. I caught the rope and opened the door and handed it to my mother, who passed it to my father, who threw it over the kidnapped tree to me, and so on five times. Then I got in front so as not to wake my sisters, and we drove home.

As was traditional, the tree was too tall by a foot, and we added another resin streak to the white ceiling. We placed it flat on the floor again.

"I'll have to saw the top off a little," Dad said. "I'll be right back." He started toward the cellar door.

"I'll get the saw," I volunteered, starting toward the door myself, hoping to trick my way into a closer glimpse at the surprise in the garage.

He paused for a split-second, then thought better of it. "No, Eddie, I'll get it. You help your mother set the table."

Almost, I thought to myself. If I had only had a little more time to "establish rapport," I might have had my chance.

My mother came down the stairs with my sisters in their pajamas, carrying the midnight blue quilt.

"Sit on the couch, girls, and get warmy. You can watch your big brother and father play with the tree." She placed them on the couch, covered them with the quilt, tucked them in.

"Get warmy," echoed my baby sister. "Watch tree."

"Need any help with setting the table?" I asked.

"Well, establishing rapport with your mother, are you?" she said. "And right before Christmas, too. Won't Santa be proud of you!"

He better be, I thought silently, *for doing a girl's job.*

"Yes, ma'am, which tablecloth should we use?" The Christmas linens were out of the cedar chest on the sideboard.

"Put on the everyday one. I'm saving the special one for when company comes on the big day."

As I finished the balancing of the tablecloth, up the stairs came my father, with the saw.

"Tablecloth's on, Mom, I'm going to help Dad with the tree," I said, getting out of work with the oldest trick in the family book, playing one parent against the other.

"All right, but could you put out some plates from the china closet?"

My father had diplomatically gone upstairs to the bathroom, to take the pressure off my housekeeping chore. Now I had no excuse. I laid out the plates

[text obscured]

my father started ... a moment my section of the tree was detached. I opened my fingers and the treetop clung for a second, then dropped onto the newspaper.

"Eddie, run downstairs and get the metal tree base and the box with the angel. They're on the cedar chest."

Downstairs and back in record time, I handed the base to my father, the box to Nancy. "Remember this?" I asked her.

"Let Mary see," said my baby sister, grabbing for the box.

Nancy drew out a simple metal winged figure, mouth open in song, holding a book. "Look, Mary," said my sister educationally, "it's an angel."

"Oooh, aindel," she said, her voice trying to reflect the specialness of the moment though unable to pronounce the word.

My mother came out of the kitchen to check our progress. "Look, Mama, aindel."

"Ooh, the angel," cooed my mother, joining the tone of the moment and accenting the soft "g" for my sister's sake. "Alvey, do you remember when we got this?"

"Sure do, our first Christmas in this house, when Nancy was the baby."

"And we couldn't afford a tree, with all the hospital bills that year, remember?" Right before my eyes, she was getting into the Christmas Spirit, a mood that officially came upon her at some point in time before the holiday. Often it coincided with the appearance of a marionette movie from Bell Telephone, but this year, it was the angel that did it.

My father, encumbered by the task of the tree, was not in the same mood.

She continued, "And then the plant gave you that pitiful bonus and you brought the angel home and said, 'Trees come and trees go, but you'll always be my angel.'"

"Aindel," echoed Mary.

"A-a-ngel, je, je," corrected Nancy.

"Aindel, de, de."

My father looked up from his work. He rose from the floor, took my mother in ballroom dance position, and they started to dance, as he sang, "I saw Mommy kissing Santa Claus…" The rapport being established was suffocating.

A sound issued from the kitchen, a hissing sound of fat burning.

"The steaks!" cried my mother, dashing out of the room. Some clattering sounds issued forth and then, "We'll eat in two minutes, I hope you're finished in there."

"We would be if we weren't so distracted by angel visits." The tone of his response and the accompanying wink soon gave me to know I had nothing to dread. He was screwing the tree into place in the stand. He moved the end table out of the corner to make room, and I helped him push the tree into position. The ceiling was six inches above the tree, leaving room for the angel.

"Mary, do you want to put the angel on top?" he asked.

"Isn't that Santa's job?" I objected, defending tradition jealously.

"Well, I think he won't mind a helper," responded my father, taking the child with the angel in his arms.

"Aindel."

"Angel," corrected Nancy.

"Anne, do you want to see this? Mary's going to put the angel on the tree."

"Coming."

securing the angel in a more balanced pose.

"Aindel," she said proudly, pointing to her handiwork.

"Angel, je, je," tutored her older sister.

"Angel," Mary said, finally.

"Yes, angel," we all cheered in unison.

"Anybody hungry?" asked my mother.

"Yes," we said, in unison again.

"Eddie, go wash your hands." I looked down at two blackened sticky hands. I'd never get this off. "Use some cold cream, that should work."

Oh, the ignominy. First setting the table, and now using my mother's cold cream.

"Come on, son," my father said. "Mine are dirty, too."

The cold cream worked. My father's participation eased the shame of it. The towel we used, however, was only good for the rag bag afterward.

Coming down the stairs, I asked him, "Dad, if we didn't have a tree that first year, where did the angel go?"

"We had a little tree, your mother was exaggerating. I got it Christmas Eve, after the crowds were gone. That same kid's father sold it to me for a quarter. Now let's go establish rapport with that steak."

After dinner we played Candyland as our parents cleared and washed the dishes; then we all watched "The Honeymooners." Mary was put to bed, and Nancy and I were allowed to stay up to help with the first batch of Christmas cookies. There were usually two nights of cookie preparation.

On this night my mother would make a batch of "refrigerator cookie" dough, her specialty. However, these cookies weren't baked until two days before the holiday, spending the time until then as long logs of nutty confection wrapped in waxed paper.

Nancy did most of the real helping. I was in it for the supervision and especially the taste test at the end. The dough of the white cookies I passed up, but the chocolate ones, never. They were of the consistency of Tootsie Rolls, only more chocolatey. I was always amazed at the process of turning ingredients that tasted bad in themselves, such as flour and raw eggs, into a mixture that tasted great. As they worked, and I watched, we talked about Christmas.

"I can't wait till next year, after I receive my first Communion in April. Next Christmas I'm going to three masses and receive communion three times," I boasted.

"You can't do that," protested my sister, "can he, Mom? Three times?"

"Can too, Sister said that on Christmas we're allowed," I responded.

"If that's what Sister said, then I guess it's true," said Mom. There was a Father/Sister/Teacher Is Always Right policy in the parish school at the time.

"Midnight Mass, seven and ten-fifteen." The church was just around the corner, so this plan was feasible. And enticing, actually. Just being in the church at that time of year was exciting. There were always scads of flowers and a crèche with half-lifesize figures above which floated angel-hair clouds against a blue velvet sky strung with lights that blinked on and off in a seemingly random pattern. During this season, I spent much of my church time watching these lights, blurring my eyes, so that I could identify the patterns like artificial constellations. If you stared long enough, and blurred well enough, it seemed that the stars were moving like teams of football players across the field of blue.

masses as I want and not

ferring my skill as teacher's per to

"Good idea," said Mom.

"Maybe we could."

Dad came in from the living room with the needle-filled newspaper for the trash. "How's the cookie crew doing?"

"Very well, we're almost finished." Four logs of dough sat rolled and waxed-papered, one more to go.

"Dad, did you play ping-pong when you were a kid?" I asked.

"Well, we had a table at the orphanage, but we could never find the ball, and sometimes the paddles disappeared."

"I wonder if Santa will bring us one, like Mary asked for today," I mused, watching his face closely for any sign of information.

He smiled broadly, "Well, he might have a surprise this year. Have you kids been good?"

"Yes, sir," came the choral answer.

"Santa is full of surprises," said my Mom. "He brought us a Christmas tree one year when we couldn't afford one."

I stole a look at my father. He grinned back.

"And I know he loves these cookies, so he just might..."

"He ate them last year," added Nancy, "and left a note."

"And surprised us with those bikes we could grow into," I added. My beautiful, unsolicited twenty-six-inch bike with blocks on the pedals so my feet would reach them was still sitting downstairs waiting for me to grow into it. Nancy's was well used, since it was a girl's and she could stand on the pedals and ride without sitting down, unobstructed by the crossbar of a boys' bike.

"So he'll probably surprise us this year with something," I said, reaching for a clue. None was forthcoming.

"Time for bed," my mother announced.

The next few days passed quickly. On the last day of school, the twenty-third, a Wednesday, Father Meyer visited each classroom and brought us each a box of candy animals. He had done the same thing the year before, and the year before that, I imagined. The animals were clear and colored like stained glass, made of barley sugar, my mother would tell us. They were not very good to eat but a sign that the holiday was here.

We gave Sister a clock for her desk, chosen by one of the parents. She said she liked it. We believed her. Nuns don't lie.

The energy of the lines leaving the school was very high. Our hearts were light, as were our bookbags. It was almost as good as summer vacation: this year we didn't come back until January 4, since January 2, the normal time for coming back, fell on a Saturday.

We had spent the last day of school finishing handmade presents for our parents. This year I made a cut-out stable scene from construction paper and lined paper, colored with crayons, then sprinkled with glitter on cotton-ball clouds glued above the birthplace of the Baby Jesus. I tried to blur my eyes to see the constellations, but it was not the same. However, judging from my mother's response the year before, I knew this would be a hit with her.

That night the house was filled with the aroma of cookies. The hibernating refrigerator cookies were sliced from the roll and laid out on the pan. But there were also chocolate chip cookies, with the one ingredient that tasted great by itself. And there were pies! Cherry, blueberry from a jar, pumpkin from a can, and apple from scratch. With some of the leftover crust, Mom made little apple turnover little

I spent Thursday, Christmas Eve, wrapping presents for my sisters and parents. We got a little extra allowance at that time of year. I had bought a clothes set and comb and mirror set for Nancy's Barbie, and a rubber whale toy for Mary. For my parents I got the things that were on the top of their lists—Old Spice aftershave for my dad and Jean Naté Bath Splash for my mom—and of course the handmade crèche.

My mother and sisters and I went to "Midnight Mass" at seven-thirty, and the constellations went wild. We said a prayer at the crèche and lit a candle.

When we got home we had cocoa with marshmallows on the dining room table, and we finally were allowed to have a cookie—but just one, because it was pretty late and we had to leave some for Santa, after all. We wrote him a note and left it under the plate, telling him to help himself to milk in the fridge, leaving a clean empty glass for this purpose, which we knew would be used by the time we came down the next morning, proving his existence in the face of big-mouth Robert Lombardo, who said there was no such thing.

The last thing we did before going to bed was hang up our special stockings under the banister. I lay awake trying to hear him coming. Then we heard sirens and were called downstairs to look out the front door, and there he was riding a fire engine down Springfield Road, with spotlights on him, waving his white gloves, and patting his big bag of toys. Then we hastened back to bed, hoping that he wouldn't forget us and that he'd have enough time to trim our tree, which had been sitting bare, except for an aluminum angel at the top, since Saturday.

I must have fallen asleep because I was awakened by the voice of my mother. "Eddie, wake up, it's Christmas." She was standing in the doorway of my room, holding Mary in her arms.

I jumped out of bed, put on my robe and slippers, and shuffled into the hall. There was a strange sound coming from downstairs—the whirring of a machine. Looking down from the top of the stairs I could see proof of Santa's visit, for there were many shadows cast by colored lights on the wall of the stairwell. The tree had been trimmed. He had come. But what was the noise?

My mother went down first, then Nancy, and I followed. Nancy's mouth fell open.

"What is it, ping-pong?" I asked. She didn't answer but ran down the stairs. I came down slowly and looked over the banister. There, on the floor, under the tree, where the couch had been, was the green board on two-by-fours, but instead of a net there were tracks and little houses, and a little conductor with a little lantern, and going round and round was a real electric train—a black engine with six cars, including a caboose, a red caboose. My father was sitting on the floor at one end of the green board working a dial on a black box. I ran down and knelt on the floor next to my sister and watched this amazing thing.

"Watch this, son," he said, as he leaned over and swiveled a switch, allowing the train to go into a middle loop, past little plastic people, past a small church with cellophane stained glass, past an iced pond made from a small round mirror, with snow on top. When the train passed a particular point in the loop, the conductor moved and waved the lantern. The engine had a headlamp that really lit. I put my head close to the track and watched it as it barreled toward

sister trying to grab it. Later in the day Barbie and Ken both took a ride in the coal car; Mary's new whale took a ride too. I learned the sweet smell of ozone that came when a piece of metal tinsel hit two tracks, or the engine stalled, and I learned how to work the transformer.

The train would be the focus of every Christmas from then on for me and my father. Setting it up each year with him was a sweet part of the holiday time. I'm not sure this present was a completely selfless one, given the joy it gave him. He wasn't a handy man, for sure—the platform would never be jacked up on sawhorses, like the Forbes'—but he sure knew how to establish rapport with a seven-year-old son who didn't play ping-pong.

Camp Columbus

Court of Honor and receive badges and pins in order to rise up through the ranks. Although mothers were an important aspect of Cub Scout life, since the weekly meetings were at the Den Mother's house, and although sisters of Scouts were invited to the Blue and Gold Banquet once a year, the institution was single-gender in its essence, like a fort. In fact, in some ways, scouting was a gentrification of the games of "Army" and "Cowboys and Indians" that we played without adult supervision. Instead of attacking the other groups, we lined up and paraded with them, but it was still a kind of moving formation. We also learned the tricks of solidarity that have been at the basis of single-gender clubs throughout history—special salutes, secret handshakes, heraldry, special gear, and of course, uniforms.

The uniforms and special gear could only be purchased at a special department of Lit Brothers, a large store downtown. The goods were almost hidden beyond the men's department—in order to get there, you had to know where you were going, another aspect of Scout training.

Once discovered, however, the place was a wonderland of tools and equipment, all chartered by the national Scout organization, most imprinted with the Scout logo. There were cases full of penknives, sheathed hunting knives, axes (hand and regular), compasses of various styles and materials, match holders (weatherproof), small velvet bags holding flint and steel for firemaking, mess kits that expanded out of a small canvas bag, canteens, and flashlights. There were racks of books, including the *Boy Scout Handbook*, on its cover the ghost of an Indian chief sitting at the campfire with uniformed lads—as well as books on Indian lore, beadmaking, leatherwork, feather work, camping, and forestry. Uniformed mannequins stood all around. This trip to Lit Brothers to order my Cub Scout uniform was a highlight of my youth.

You couldn't just go and pick one up. No, these uniforms were so special they had to be tailored to fit each individual boy. Walking into that area beyond the cases to be measured made me feel very grown up. As we approached the mirrors, a man with a white shirt and tie, a yellow measuring tape hanging around his neck, appeared from a doorway I had not noticed.

"Well, another scouting customer…Let me guess—Explorer, right?"

"No, sir…"

"Don't tell me, Eagle Scout, right?"

"No, sir, I'm working on my Wolf Badge. I'm only a Cub Scout."

"Well, you're awful big for a Cub Scout. Step up on the stage here, young man, and let's see what your shirtsleeve is."

I stepped up onto a wooden box. He held my arm out straight and measured shoulder to wrist.

"Shall we leave a little sleeve to grow into?" he asked my mother.

"Oh, yes, please." The uniforms were expensive, I figured from the tone of her voice. The man took a little pad from his pocket and made some notes on it.

"Now, Parade Rest!" the man ordered.

We had just learned this stance the week before. I stood with my legs apart, placing my arms behind me.

"Very good, young man, not everybody that comes in here knows their manual. What pack are you in?"

I resumed my open-legged position. "You surprised me, that's all."

"Inseam, nineteen, shall I leave a little?"

"Please," said my mother.

The man went on to measure my waist and outseam—even my head, for the Cub Scout hat. Then he handed my mother a piece of paper, telling her to take it to the cash register to pay.

"A week to ten days is all it should take."

For the next week, I ran home after school every day. Nothing. It wasn't until two Saturdays later, when I was home watching "Ramar of the Jungle" on television, that I heard the knock on the door. When I opened it, I saw a man with a box with the word LITS emblazoned on the front.

"Stivender?"

"That's us."

"Sign here."

I signed the paper on his clipboard and took the package. I knew what it was. I ripped open the packaging and then the box. The smell hit me before I saw it. New clothes. *New* new clothes. Made for me, only to fit *me*. There is no smell like it. I rifled through the tissue paper and uncovered the treasure. Dark blue one hundred percent cotton twill, with brass buttons and yellow fluting. *Cub Scouts of America* above the right pocket of the shirt. Quickly I took my shirt off and put on the new one. The sleeves were too long. They went to my fingertips.

Now I had to make a choice. I could send it back and wait another two or even three weeks, or accept what I had received and make the best of it.

"Eddie, who was at the door?" my mother called from upstairs.

"The man from Lit Brothers with my uniform."

"Wonderful, does it fit?"

"Not sure yet," I hedged, trying to decide what to do.

I tried on the pants. They were a little loose at the waist, but the length was pretty good. The belt had a shiny brass buckle. I put it through the loops and tightened it, my hands sometimes getting caught in the sleeves of the shirt. Out of the box fell two patches, one saying SPRINGBROOK, the other, *261*. I picked the patches up and turned them over in my hands, reverently. I was really a Cub Scout now. Long sleeves or not, no way this uniform was going back.

I folded the cuff back just one time and buttoned it, then did the same with the other. The extra layer made the cuff tight at my wrist so it didn't slide down. Perfect. Now I could grow into it. I wouldn't have to get another uniform until I entered Boy Scouts.

I only saw one other thing in the box, the neckerchief. I unfolded it and put it flat on the couch, then carefully began to roll it from the widest part of the triangle halfway to the point with the logo. I put it over my shoulders. I heard my mother coming down the stairs.

"Not yet, Mom, I don't have it all on yet, don't come down."

She paused on the third step and waited as I went through the tissue for the neckerchief slide, a metal ring with a rendering of a turk's head knot that kept the two long ends of the kerchief together at the neck. It was in the corner of the box. Hands shaking from the pressure of my mother waiting on the stairs, I pushed the two corners through and

"You'll grow into it, unless you want to send it back?"

"No, I like it this way," I said, to convince myself as much as her. "Here're the patches, can you sew them on before Monday night?"

"I don't know why not."

"Good, I'm going next door and show the Halls."

"Wait a minute, where's your hat?" She lifted up the lid and produced the hidden beanie. It fit perfectly, which meant that I would probably grow out of it soon.

That afternoon was spent showing off my new uniform to the neighborhood. The next Monday night I wore my newly patched Springbrook 261 blues to the meeting. My Pledge of Allegiance was prouder and louder, my Cub Scout Oath more sincere, and my salutes sharper than ever before.

That night was special for another reason. A representative of the Knights of Columbus was there to invite us to attend a summer camp that they ran in New Jersey. For only twenty dollars per week, a Catholic Cub Scout could learn to swim, do arts and crafts, tie knots, and play Indian in the fresh air of the Jersey Pines. He showed slides of the lake with happy boys swimming and canoeing, slides of the parade grounds with the same boys raising and saluting the flag, slides of the mess hall with the same boys eating and waving, slides of the archery range, and so forth.

It looked good to me. I got a brochure and, when I got home, started my campaign of begging my parents to let me go. It was not the lake that attracted me—I was scared to death of the water; but a camp with all boys seemed like the ultimate fort experience. A chance to get away from my sisters and be a wild child, like the boys in *Peter Pan.*

Forts had been important to me for as long as I can remember. Across the street from our house was a field that for some reason the developer had left untouched, perhaps sensing its future commercial value. In the center of the three-acre lot was a little hollow with an auspicious grouping of rocks, which served as seats of honor for our tribal meetings. There were paths going out from the rocks in three directions through chest-high weeds. The field was a textbook sampler of Northeastern flora. There was Queen Anne's lace, thistle, at least two kinds of milkweed, all sorts of weeds with stickers that would attach to clothing, and most important of all, a stand of dockweed that ran along the whole streetside length of the lot.

Dockweed, found throughout the Northeast, has large leaves at the top of bamboo-like hollow stalks. The roots are shallow, making the stalks easy to pull out of the ground. These are good to use as spears, as the roots are pointed when cleaned of soil, and the hollowness of the stalks makes them light so that they are easy to throw but hardly dangerous. Getting one's eye knocked out with such a weapon is possible, I suppose, but not likely.

What makes a good fort? A hidden entrance, known only to the members of the fort club. Tunnels connecting the main room to other smaller rooms where stuff like spears and sharpened sticks could be stored in case of attack by strangers, or girls. Places within the fort where it was possible to see the outside world, including our parents across the street when they called us in for dinner.

Dockweed is a perfect matrix for such a fort. It is easy for us was the ease with which we could create tunnels through the stand of stalks, since the leaves were large and dense. And the previous year's stalks could be used as matting for the present year's floor.

Our fort club was made up of most of the boys on our block. From the time I was allowed to cross the street, at age seven, I would go to the field with my friends. We would play war games, hold spear-throwing contests, bury dead cats killed on Springfield Road, then dig them up months later to look at the remains. It was wonderful.

I expected that Camp Columbus would be a fort writ large, so my campaign of begging lasted until my parents said yes. The next day Michael Hall, my next-door neighbor and fort buddy, told me his parents had agreed as well. We would be going together, the same week. All told, five kids from my pack would be going at the same time.

Preparation for camp was exciting. Usually I would get new underwear and T-shirts whenever we went on vacation, but this year I got extras. In addition my father had sent away for a ribbon of ID tags, and my mother sewed my name into every article of clothing so that nothing would get lost. I also got new sneakers, P.F. Flyers, which the ads on television claimed could make you "run faster and jump higher." I ran home with them under my arm, my old Keds on my feet. My new sneakers smelled deliciously new as I took them out of the box, and as I slipped them on I thought, *Last time they're gonna smell like this.*

As I laced them I knew they would work, even if it was only the "feather effect" I had recently seen on the cartoon *Dumbo.* I went out back and called up to the Bates's and Forbes's windows, challenging the neighborhood kids to a race around the block. I beat everyone but Gregory Bates, but he had P.F. Flyers as well so I didn't feel too bad.

So it was that one Saturday in July I packed my gear into my father's duffel bag from the service, threw it in the trunk of the Plymouth Cedarwood, and off I went to camp, sitting in the back seat with Mike, singing songs and playing license tag games. Over the bridge and into Jersey, past the turnoff to my cousins' house, and on and on into the Jersey Pines, many thousand acres with not much in the way of population or civilization.

We finally turned off the road onto a gravel drive marked by an old sign nailed to a tree that read CAMP COLUMBUS. This back road was longer than I expected, and very bumpy, me and Mike standing with our hands gripping the upholstery of the front seat as we bounced. We pulled up to a sandlot full of cars. People were streaming toward a building with a large chimney. Beyond that we could see rows of smaller buildings, and beyond them a lake gleamed in the sunlight.

We got our gear out of the trunk and started toward the gathering crowd on the lawn in front of the main building. Over to the side were a few smaller clusters of people. As I got closer I saw that these were families gathered around prematurely homesick campers. Some would abandon their boys, letting them become the original "unhappy campers."

For the first time I felt afraid, although I wasn't sure why. I had stayed overnight at my cousins' house, so I didn't expect to get homesick, but this was the first time with so many strangers. I recognized Armand d'Agostino, from down Springfield Road, and I waved. He waved back and

on either side of him were high school-aged guys—the counselors, I figured. The short man blew the whistle. We all quieted, except the kid next to Armand, who soon was whisked away by his mother, the first casualty of the event. I felt sorry for the kid but better when he was out of earshot. Crying is contagious, as anyone with sisters can tell you.

"Welcome to Camp Columbus," said the man to the quieted crowd. "I am Mr. Ricci, the camp director and swimming instructor."

Swimming. I suddenly remembered why I was scared. I wondered what technique he would use with us. I was hoping it did not include going in water over my head, or even putting my head into shallow water. I fought the urge to grasp my mother's hand. He continued.

"These are the counselors who will be supervising your boys this week." He introduced them by name. None looked dangerous, though some were bigger than others. One had a snake around his neck, showing off. Then he gestured deferentially to a man in a short-sleeved black shirt and Roman collar. "This is our chaplain, Father Deegan. There will be Mass every morning, and if any boy wishes to go to Confession, Father is available by appointment." It was the first time I had ever seen a priest's bare arms. But we were in

Jersey, and everybody knew it was more lax here. He didn't look much older than the counselors, though shorter and better groomed. Perhaps I would use his services before swimming lest I drown without confessing my sins first.

"I want you parents to know the boys will be in good hands, and next week, when you come back to pick them up, they will be a little browner, a little healthier, and a little more skillful. The list of boys and their respective cabins is on the announcement board behind you, as well as the schedule for the week, in case you're interested. If you have any questions, I'll be available for a little while here on the porch. Thanks for coming, and for being smart enough to send your boy to the best camp on the East Coast. Good day."

We all rushed to the board to find our cabin number. I'd be in Cabin 6, Mike was in Cabin 7, right next door. Bad luck that we weren't together, but at least he wouldn't be too far away.

"This way, you'll make new friends, both of you," said my father.

"Yeah," we both said halfheartedly, as we made our way to the cabins. In front of Cabin 6 was a teenager with a crewcut and a Villanova T-shirt. In front of Cabin 7 stood the guy with the snake.

"Congratulations, Mike," I kidded. "Check your sleeping bag before you go to sleep tonight."

"Very funny."

I approached the cabin where I would spend the next seven nights. The counselor saw me coming, his first charge, apparently.

"What's your name, Scout?"

"Ed Stivender, Springbrook two-sixty-one."

"Right." He checked it off. "You're the first one here, so you get to choose your bunk. Mine's the one on the bottom by the door. My name is Bill Murphy. I'm your counselor."

I entered the cabin, leaving my parents outside to talk to my counselor. It was lit by a bare bulb in the center of the room. Five steel-frame bunk beds stood in a random pattern. I chose the one in the corner closest to Cabin 7, in the back. I put my stuff on the lower bunk and went outside to say

like a baby like the kid who had cried his way out of staying, but I wasn't sure this was as good as the fort across the street from my house in Westbrook Park. Before they were out of sight I turned back to the cabin where some of the campers were still hugging their parents. It occurred to me that Mike was lucky, saying goodbye to his parents before he got into the car with us. I looked over to his cabin, and there he was, taking a turn holding the snake. He looked up at me and made a weird face like a native in a Tarzan movie. I laughed, forgetting about my parents, and joined my mates in front of the cabin.

Bill Murphy took roll and explained how we would spend the week. There would be an inspection of the cabin every day. We were expected to have our bunks made and gear stowed by the time the flag was raised, at eight o'clock.

"I'd like to get the Honor Cabin ribbon at least two times this week, so you guys are going to have to put in a little bit of extra effort." The Honor Cabin ribbon went to the cabin that was neatest and best swept. I liked the idea of working together on something so tangible and frequently rewarded. I had learned at school to use a push broom, which stood in a corner of the cabin near the door. This part would be a snap.

He explained the rest of his expectations, went over the daily schedule, then asked if there were any questions.

A chubby kid raised his hand. "Is there a candy store in the camp?"

A good question, we all agreed. My father had given me a couple of dollars for spending money.

"After dinner every night, the PX will be open. They have sodas and candy. But the meals are pretty filling, so nobody goes hungry."

I raised my hand. "Do we have to take the swimming class?"

"Everybody has to take at least one swim a day. If you know how to swim and pass the swimming test, you don't have to take a class. Beginners go with Mr. Ricci, intermediates with Joe Smith, advanced are on their own."

Rats, I thought, no way out.

"All right, one more thing. There's a show on Friday night. If you have a talent, sign up with me and you can be in the show."

Another hand went up. "I know hambone, if anybody wants to learn." The speaker had a Southern accent and was a little older than the rest of us. Some of the kids laughed.

"Hambone?" asked Bill.

"Yeah," the Southern kid continued. "It's using your body like a drum, like this." He crouched and began to slap his hands against his thighs and chest, making a remarkable sound. When he was finished, we all applauded.

"All right," said Bill, "you have about an hour before dinner. Make yourselves at home, walk around, when you hear the bell, report to the building with the big chimney. That's the Mess Hall."

I went back inside the cabin to roll out my sleeping bag. The boy in the bunk above me had already done so and was relaxing.

"Afraid to swim, hunh?" he asked.

"No, I'm not, what gave you that idea?"

"Oh, nothing, just guessing."

I focused on my bedroll, my ears burning. When I was finished I stood straight and looked at him. "How about you, you afraid to swim?"

water. Lots of kids are. You probably have other stuff you're good at."

"I like to run."

"Good. How about tetherball?"

I had never heard of it. "I'm not sure, how do you play?"

He jumped down off the bunk. "Follow me." I followed him across the parade ground to a pole to which a soccer ball was attached with a leather line. "You stand on this side of the pole," he said, moving to the other side and taking the ball in his hands, "and I stand on this side, and we each try to wrap the ball line around the pole while keeping the other guy from doing it. Watch, don't stop it this time."

He gave the ball a whack and it flew around, just over my head, and continued to make smaller and smaller circles until it could go no further.

"Oh, I get it," I said, pushing the ball in the other direction so we could start over.

Tetherball turned out to be great fun, and soon Mike came over and we played teams with my bunkmate and the Southern kid. The hour went quickly, and soon the dinner bell called us into the Mess Hall. I sat at the table with my cabinmates. The food was pretty good, but the "bug juice" that served for a beverage tasted like brand-X punch. After supper the camp was divided into two teams for a game of "Capture the Flag." It was a wild game, with too many kids for it to make much sense, but it took our minds off the approach of our first night away from home.

As promised, the PX opened, and I got M&Ms and a Coke. I showed off to my new friends, making scuba divers of the M&Ms by dropping them in one at a time and shaking the bottle. The colored candies fell to the bottom then rose with carbonation, right on cue. I had learned the trick from *The Book of Knowledge,* an ancient encyclopedia at my grandmothers'. At eight o'clock we went to the auditorium for cartoons. When we walked out it was dark, and we had to use flashlights to get back to our cabins.

We were in bed a little before ten, when the lights went out and Taps was played. I promised myself I was not going to cry. I almost kept my promise, but when I heard a whimper from the chubby kid, I lost it for a second. Only one tear managed to escape, running across my cheek; when it entered my ear, I stopped. I turned on my side and tried to see through a chink in the wall, but I couldn't distinguish anything in the dark. I shimmied deeper into the sleeping bag and fell asleep.

You gotta get up, you gotta get up, you gotta get up this morning. I had heard Reveille in cartoons, but it was the first time I had ever heard it in person. I jumped onto the cold wood floor and made my bed, grabbed my soap kit and towel, and ran out the door toward the latrines to wash up. We had fifteen minutes before inspection to do it all. The facilities were fairly modern, with running hot and cold water and toilets that flushed, but the bathroom was more public than the one at home. There, you lined up outside the door and waited for whomever was inside to finish, giving periodic cues with your hand on the door. Here, everybody was inside, jostling to take turns at the various facilities.

I was happy with my speed and efficiency. I was the first boy back in the cabin, so I got to sweep the floor. Though the broom was like the one at school, the dirt was

through the trees behind me, making long shadows of the tall pines. I was joined by my new friends, and we all stood at attention watching the flag ceremony in the middle of the field. After that, Mr. Ricci came around and inspected all the cabins. Cabin 2 received the ribbon of honor.

After breakfast we had Crafts. I went to the lanyard group. A lanyard is a woven length of twine made of leather—or in our case, plastic—thongs, usually with a metal hook at the end to hold a whistle or keys or a penknife. As I discovered that day, there were several different designs, yielding different shapes and patterns. I learned two styles and made a watch fob in green and silver as I thought about what was coming after lunch—swimming. I don't know where my fear of the water had originated. Whatever the reason, I was sure that I would drown someday. This might be the day.

We lined up on the beach. The water was brown from all the cedars surrounding it, and it smelled very sweet. Mr. Ricci took us through a series of exercises to warm us up and get us in the mood. Then he invited us to come over to the deepest part and stand by the railings to see him demonstrate the technique of floating. The railings were thick wood posts and I grasped one hard and looked over into ten feet of water as he jumped in. As soon as his head was out of the water he began to speak, telling us over and over how easy and undangerous it really was. I felt sure he had a skill I didn't have—or perhaps a genetic trait that allowed him to float better.

"The water is your friend, boys. It wants to hold you up, you just have to let it. Watch me as I let my arms float out to my sides as I put my head back and float. My face is out of the water and I can just relax and take it easy, see?"

He climbed the ladder onto the pier. "Now boys, everybody in up to their waist." I put my name-tagged towel on the sand and approached my murderer. For the first two yards sand had been replaced by small stones from the lapping of the tiny waves. *At least there're no crabs,* I thought, trying to encourage myself, not too successfully. The water was cool and seemed to get colder as it neared my "sea anchor." At least we were all beginners, and the spirit of apprehension was shared; but drowning, I knew, was something you did by yourself.

"Now fellas, crouch down so it's up to your shoulders," came the director's voice behind us. We obeyed with varying degrees of enthusiasm. I was shivering. I began to say the Hail Mary to myself, knowing that whistling a happy tune was inappropriate and in fact impossible between blue lips. I calmed down enough to keep the level of water at my neck.

"Now, when I say three, everybody duck their head into the water. I want to see everybody's head wet when you come up. One, two, three."

I closed my eyes and let my knees go. Felt the moment of panic and stood up, rubbing my eyes clear so that I could see. I had done it.

"Very good, boys, now everybody turn around and walk out to the rope."

We all made our way to the blue and white rope with plastic buoys that separated the shallow from the deep. On the other side was my enemy the deep. The water was now up to my neck. I grabbed the rope.

"Now, boys, hang on to the rope and float with your head out of the water."

I knew that this was impossible. If I had been alone on one foot up and kept one foot in the sand, I got the hang of it. The secret was not to depend on the rope for support. I could only do it for a few seconds at a time before I stood up, but Mr. Ricci apparently didn't notice, such was the chaos in the water. Then I started trying it without the rope, using my hands in front of me for balance and buoyancy. I was doing it. Sort of swimming! If only for a few seconds at a time.

"All right boys, that's enough for today, you can have a few minutes' free time before the other boys come down for regular swim."

Not me, I thought, *I don't need no free time.* I walked out of the lake and onto the beach over to my towel and sat down. I was panting but proud. My fingernails were blue. I knew my lips were too. I dried my head and face and lay back on the sand, using the towel as my pillow. The sky was bluer than at home. *Good to be alive,* I thought, meaning, *Glad I didn't drown.*

The rest of the swimming lessons that week were bearable. I got used to the food, and our cabin won the ribbon of honor on Wednesday. I was looking forward to Thursday morning, however, because we were going to take an "Indian Brave

Run" through the woods. From what I could gather, this event was a double-time march for the whole camp, half going down one trail, the other half down another. Running was something I could do, and I wanted to try out my new P.F.s, so I was excited about the prospect.

About an hour after breakfast on Thursday, we all lined up with our counselors by the flagpole.

"Now boys," shouted Mr. Ricci, "this run is a tradition here at Camp Columbus. The first thing to remember is, go at your own pace and don't get overheated. If you run out of breath or get a stitch in your side, slow down, and walk if you have to. Counselors will bring up the rear so no one gets lost or left behind."

I heard a sigh of relief from the chubby kid. It occurred to me that he was as afraid of this as I had been of swimming. This balance in nature made me thankful. I was tempted to say something to him but knew how stupid encouragement always sounded to me, so I refrained.

"On your mark, get set, go."

Our counselor, Bill, and Chip, the counselor who had had the snake the first day, were to be at the front of the pack. The snake stayed home. A couple of kids ran very quickly ahead of us, even the counselors, but they got winded, and we caught up to them in a few minutes. The group was beginning to filter itself into positions of enthusiasm and foot-dragging. I stayed close to the counselors. I felt that with my new sneaks, I could outrun the pack of them, maybe even the counselors, who were discussing the John Wayne movie, *Wake of the Red Witch,* the last scene of which has the hero drowning in a diving suit. It made me nervous, so I moved ahead of them, not winded at all, my soles digging into the sandy trail. I pretended I was indeed an Indian brave, a scout in fact, running before my tribe, looking for game or enemies.

Being an Indian was of great value in the scouting mythos. One of my spring projects had been the production of a breechclout with animal symbols that I wore at the final Court of Honor for the year. We had danced around a pretend fire over which I bravely jumped, whooping wildly.

much, I figured, and I slowed to their pace, still ahead of the rest. I was surprised that I was at the front, not overheated, not even out of breath. I pushed forward a little, hoping that they'd pick up the pace. They did for a bit, then the other counselor puffed, "Bill, let's stop and wait for the rest."

They halted, but I kept going.

"Hey, Ed, come back here and sit down. We're going to hold up for the rest of the kids," shouted Bill. I turned around and jogged back, turning my run into another dance, and sang a song to the tune we had used at the Court of Honor:

Hey hey hey hey,
Once there was a Brave,
His moccasins could fly,
He outran all the others,
Lightfoot was his name,
Hey Hey Hey.

I was elated. It was wonderful to be able to do something outside of schoolwork better than anybody else. The counselors were sitting beneath a great pine tree, the others were straggling up the road. I sat down on the soft needles.

My campmates were beginning to arrive. I was pleased to see that the chubby kid from my cabin was not the last to show up. The last kid was limping and would have to be taken back with a sprained ankle by one of the counselors.

"What took you guys so long?" I taunted the Southern kid.

"Didn't want to show you Yankees up, is all," he panted, sitting down next to me.

"Listen up, everybody," said Bill. "We're about halfway there. Is everybody feeling OK?"

Grunts and groans from the crowd.

"We're gonna take five here. Anybody needs to go to the bathroom, go over there, number one only, anything else hold it in." More grunts and groans. A few kids walked over to the designated place. I took my sneakers off and emptied them of sand and gravel. They really did make me run faster, or at least longer.

When it came time to begin again, Chip spoke. "Listen up, we're gonna take it easy going back. First I'd like to announce the Brave of the Run, the boy who ran the best the longest. It's this kid here." He pointed to me.

"Ed, my name is Ed," I said proudly, peeved that he hadn't asked me first.

"Ed, his name is Ed, but his Indian name is Lightfoot." Some halfhearted cheers from my tribe. "Lightfoot will help take up the rear on the way home, now let's get started."

Mike Hall came over and patted me on the back. "Lightfoot, eh? Didn't know you had an Indian name."

"I just made it up."

As we headed back to camp, I tried to figure out what had just happened. Was I really Brave of the Run, or had they invented it? Was taking up the rear a punishment for running too fast, or a real honor? To this day I don't know. What I do know is that on some level this made up for my fear of the lake. I held my head high as I walked to the rears, *primus inter pares,* first among equals, fulfilling the New Testament reading for the day—"The first shall be last."

Walking at the rear was pretty interesting, anyway. I learned the chest-slapping part of hambone. Later that night, after dinner, I learned the thigh part, and on Friday night I

After the talent show we sang the camp song one last time.

Hail O Hail O Camp Columbus,
In the Jersey Pines—

The tune was "Hail, Columbia," but we didn't know that then.

The next morning, right after breakfast, we gathered in front of the Mess Hall for a camp picture. I still have it. Mr. Ricci in the middle, next to Father Deegan, the rest of us lined up in rows, sitting, kneeling, standing. Behind us the counselors, one with a snake. Me sitting at the end of the front row, P.F. Flyers on my feet, not afraid of nothin', ready to go home.

*M*y father was orphaned at the age of seven. His brothers and sisters were parceled out to aunts and uncles throughout the state of South Carolina, but he, runt of the litter, was turned over to the Charleston Home for Orphans and Foundlings. There he learned the ways of the world until his early retirement at the age of seventeen, when he joined the Navy.

Desiring his son to have the things he had not had—in particular, financial independence—he set me up in business at the tender age of eight, bankrolling a venture that would allow me to see the world differently from my third-grade peers.

One Friday evening he returned from work with a large paper bag containing something that rattled. He put it on the dining room table and announced, "Eddie, this is for you. It cost about ten dollars, but you don't have to pay me back right away." A strange thing to say to a boy my age: a present, but not exactly. It was my introduction to American capitalism.

I ripped the paper down the side, revealing a gray steel open toolbox with a black rubber tread above two bins that contained various supplies. I recognized that it was a deluxe shoeshine kit. It was filled with three tins of Kiwi shoe polish—black, tan, and oxblood; two beaver bristle applicator brushes; a bottle of black and a bottle of orange liquid; several sturdy cotton shine cloths; and two magnificent buffing brushes with thick natural bristles and large curved varnished wooden handles.

Trying to muster enthusiasm, I said, "Gee, thanks, Dad. It's really great." But in fact, I was confused. A few months earlier, working on a badge for Cub Scouts, I had promised my father that I would shine my shoes every night, as he had done since his Navy days. The equipment sitting before me, however, was way beyond my personal needs. I waited for his explanation.

"I spoke to Ernie and Sam at the barber shop the other day, and they said you could shine shoes there after school and on Saturdays," he said enthusiastically.

"Really?" I said, trying to sound excited, not sure what it was going to mean. The barber shop was located three blocks up the Springfield Road hill, a couple of doors down from Yeager's Bakery, near where my friend Jackie Woulfe lived. I went there every two weeks for a haircut. They had three red leather and steel barber chairs with hand-pumped hydraulic lifts, mirrors all around, red vinyl and chrome waiting chairs, and tables full of hunting and fishing magazines. On Saturdays they were always crowded; my father obviously had figured out I could do a brisk business then.

"You'll have to pay them a kind of rent, of course," he continued.

Rent, I thought to myself, my confusion increasing.

"Your rent won't be money, though, you'll pay your way by sweeping the hair off the floor."

Oh. Great.

"They said you could start tomorrow."

"Oh, great, I can start tomorrow. That sounds really neat ...," I heard myself say, bidding goodbye to the Saturday morning touch football game with the neighborhood boys.

"Now if I were you, young man, I'd get started prac-

"That's for cleaning the shoe first, before you polish."

"Oh. Neat."

I put the bottle back in its place, a little overwhelmed by the possibilities. I had never had shoes that were dirty enough to use pre-polish cleaner on, but I would definitely learn how to use the stuff. Pleasing my father was a very high priority for me.

Grabbing the kit by the tread bridge, I lifted it off the table and started up the stairs to my room to practice. It was fairly heavy, but I found I could hold it in my right hand if I balanced it against my leg as I walked. I started in on my oldest pair of shoes, from first grade, learning the technique of the cleaning step as I went. The applicator brushes were larger than the toothbrush I normally used, they took the polish better and had a larger surface. The buffing brushes took some getting used to, heavy as they were. But after three pairs of shoes, I was getting the hang of it.

When I was finished, I lay back on the bed and tried to imagine what the kids at school would say when I told them I had a job. A real job. They'd be jealous, of course, of my financial independence. There was to be a party at Mary Shillington's house in Colonial Park next weekend. I could brag then.

I started to plan how I would spend the money I was going to make. At that time I was receiving an allowance of twenty-five cents a week, enough to buy a soft pretzel or a candy bar a day, except during Lent, when I would give most of the money to the Missions to ransom pagan babies for Christ. A way to make my newfound riches stretch, however, would be found at the penny candy counter at Yeager's Bakery.

Although it was called a bakery, no baking was ever done there. Every morning Mr. Yeager would drive his wood-paneled station wagon down to who knew where, the city, probably, and return with trays of doughnuts—sugared, glazed, and jelly-filled; cinnamon sticks for five cents apiece; and cupcakes—chocolate, vanilla, strawberry-iced—also five cents. There were strange delicious cakes shaped like long pup tents; deluxe cupcakes coated with raspberry jelly, laden with coconut, and topped with a dollop of dark chocolate; large sugar cookies; and delicious-looking pies in tins for which Mr. Yeager required a deposit until returned. But the main attraction of Yeager's Bakery was the penny candy. A cornucopia of penny candy.

The candy was displayed in open boxes inside a strong kid-proof glass case that was higher than I was until fifth grade. On the upper shelves were the nickel candy bars (fifty cents today), but on the bottom shelf, visible to the shortest toddler's eyes, were caramel swirls, spearmint leaves, orange peels (hard gelatin-like chunks), chocolate caramels, black and red licorice, Red Hots, banana slices (almost pure sugar, eating one made you dizzy), jawbreakers (layers and layers of different colored hard sugar—like a gumball that yielded no gum), Tootsie Roll Pops (I began to understand the fragility of American civilization when these went up to two cents), Mary Janes, mini Tootsie Rolls, wax bottle candy (filled with colored sugar water), pill strips (dots of candy on paper—the precursor of the drug problem in America today), pumpkin seeds, Lik'm Aids (Kool-aid taken dry), and B.B. Bats (paddles of Turkish taffy and chocolate, strawberry, and banana).

Mr. and Mrs. Yeager's days were filled with stooping and rising in response to the children of Westbrook Park's

M&M's, or a Bonomo's Turkish Taffy. It would cost me five cents, but I'd be rich.

"Eddie—time to eat." The voice of my mother woke me from my financial planning. It was time for dinner. I put my newly shined shoes on and went downstairs.

"Look at the shine on them shoes," said my dad. "A real professional job."

Why not, I thought. I was becoming a real professional.

At nine-thirty the next morning we started up the hill to the shop. When we got there, the place was already busy. Ernie and Sam each had a customer, and a couple of men were waiting, reading.

"Ernie, Sam, this is my son Eddie."

"Hi, Eddie," said Ernie.

"Hi, Eddie, let me show you where the broom is. You don't have to start sweeping yet, though." Sam led me to a door handle next to a mirror on the wall. When he turned the handle, sure enough the wall opened, revealing a closet in the paneling. He flicked on a light, and I saw boxes of barber supplies, a utility sink, some rags, and a push broom of the style used at school.

"You can wait a little while, till the hair piles up a little more," said my new boss.

My father mercifully exited, taking some of the pressure off. It was time to begin. My heart racing, I took a deep breath and approached a man sitting against the back wall. I planned to make an orderly sweep of the waiting customers. I had rehearsed my two-word pitch since the night before.

"Shine, sir?"

"No thanks, sonny," he replied, looking over his magazine. Fighting the urge to drop the kit and run after my father, I went to the next man.

"Shine, sir?"

His response was more promising. "How much is it?"

"Only a dime, sir," I responded, pointing to the sign written in Magic Marker on the side of the gray kit.

"Sounds fair enough. Do you have brown?"

I put down my case and knelt on the tile. "Sure do," I said, reaching in the case and pulling out the tin to prove it.

The man placed his slightly scuffed tan shoe on the black rubber ribbing and went back to his paper, leaving me to my work. I didn't have to use the cleaning fluid, but I brushed off the invisible dust with the horsehair brush, then rolled up his cuff two rolls.

I took a penny from my pocket, put it in the space between the top and bottom of the tin, and twisted. Nothing happened. My hands were shaking, and I tried again. The top held fast. *If only his shoes were black,* I thought to myself. I knew the black tin would open, I'd gone through that struggle the night before.

I tried again, and again. The penny slipped out of my sweating fingers and rolled down the tile past the next two chairs. I could feel my face turning red as I chased the coin and retrieved it.

Resuming my kneeling position in front of my customer, thankful that he had not tried to help me, afraid to look to see if he was aware of the difficulties I was having, I said a prayer to my patron saint, Edward the Confessor,

King of England, known to have the "touch" that cured palsy in his subjects. Miraculously, the top gave way and dropped to the floor. The scent of shoe polish filled my nostrils.

I reached into the box and produced the unused brown brush. First I shmushed the brush tip around the top of the

gasp of surprise was audible when I saw the thin tan line appear on my victim's sock. I silently pledged to be more careful in the future. (This would be the major difficulty in my new job. The darker the sock, the less serious the problem. I did finally learn how to do it by trial and error. But I can still see the line on my first client's sock.)

When the shoe was completely covered with the paste, I brushed it, then took the rolled buff cloth and started to buff. Presently I flipped the cloth to the soft felt side and continued. Finally I spit on the toe of the shoe and buffed it to a high gloss. A spit shine. I hit the bottom of the sole of the shoe as a signal to change position and, my client having done so, started on the other shoe, being extra careful at the sock line.

This part went more smoothly, and two minutes later I was done. Tapping the shoe, I proudly said, "Finished, sir."

The man looked down at his shoes and smiled. "Nice job, young man. Here's fifteen cents."

"Thank you, sir," I replied, trying to hide my excitement at a job fairly well done, with a fifty percent tip to boot.

Just then Sam spoke. "You can give the floor a once-over now, Eddie."

I rose and went to the closet, got out the push broom and began, learning the moves of the dance I would do for the next several months, edging around the stationary bases of the hydraulic barber chairs, waiting for the working barber to move so I could collect the hair under his feet, then moving on to the next one, until the floor was clean of hair except for the pile I had made, which I proceeded to push into the closet, where it grew to a massive pillow by the end of the day, to be finally disposed of by Ernie or Sam. I was never sure how.

At the end of the day I had sixty-five cents in my pocket, more than two weeks' allowance, and dirty hands but a glad heart. What I would tell the kids at Mary Shillington's party. I was a working man and only eight years old.

A few doors up was Yeager's Bakery. I went in and bought a bag of M&Ms. There was a music store in the same row, and I looked in the window. There were some band instruments, a guitar, some rattles and maracas, and in the middle of the display was a pink-marbled thing that looked like a ray gun, but with finger holes. I figured it was some kind of flute. Its box was right above it with the words OCARINA and *Old-Fashioned Sweet Potato,* and the sticker on it read, *35¢.*

I still had sixty cents in my pocket, and I could sure use an instrument like that. When I saw the words *Instructions Included,* I was sold. Through the glass door and into the shop I went.

"Do you have any old-fashioned sweet potatoes?" I asked the bespectacled owner, as though I knew what I was talking about.

"Why, yes, I think we do," said the man, and reached into a glass case which held several sizes. "Which key would you prefer?" he asked, his hand heading toward a large red one.

I didn't know what a key was, but I knew the larger ones would be beyond by current budget, so I said, "What key is the one in the window?"

He brought out a box almost identical to the one in the window but unbleached by the sun. "These smaller ones are

Santa Claus, or my parents, or a prize for being smart or good. A purchase of my own—a musical instrument. I would learn to play it from the easy instructions inside the red, white, and blue box, and I would play it next Sunday after dinner for the family, but especially for my father, who had been so pleased by my performance on a toy piano a few years earlier that he had hinted at getting a real piano so I could take lessons. But the piano was long in coming, and with an ocarina I wouldn't have to wait.

"This one is thirty-five cents. Do you know how to play it?" he asked benignly.

"Instructions come with it, don't they?" I replied, perhaps a little defensively.

"Of course, but all you have to remember is, all finger holes covered is the lowest note, all holes open is the highest note. And on this one both of them are C."

"So how would you start 'Swanee River'"—the piece that had been such a hit on the toy piano two years earlier—"with two fingers raised, right?"

"Right."

Yeah, but which two, the two at the top or the two at the bottom? I thought to myself but didn't ask for fear I would end up owing him for a music lesson (which was how he made his living really, the store being a front of sorts). "I'll take it."

"That'll be thirty-six cents."

"I thought it was thirty-five cents."

"One cent for the governor."

It made me think of the Peter's Pence collection at church where we were expected to give a penny to the Pope. I was somewhat dismayed when I realized that I wouldn't have a quarter in my pocket to take home after this surprise tax, but there was no backing down now. I put the two quarters on the counter, and slipped the ocarina into my pocket.

He rang it up and gave me fourteen cents change. "We also have harmonicas that come with instructions."

"Thanks, I may be back," I said, and went out into the late afternoon sun.

I slipped the ocarina out of the box and put the box in my pocket, without even glancing at the free instructions. The thing was hard marbled plastic, with a thumb hole marked *T* and whistle hole on one side, and seven finger holes on the other side. The handle, shaped like that of a Flash Gordon ray gun, was pierced at the bottom and served as the mouthpiece.

I put that part between my lips and blew. Sure enough, a whistle came through. I laughed with nervousness and joy, a little thrilled with myself. I tried to get my fingers in the proper places, and blew again. This time the sound was not pleasant.

Then I tried to place my fingers tighter on the holes while blowing and reached a tone that felt like music. A deep tone, with a feeling of a calliope at the circus. That would be the low C. Then I blew again, with only the thumb hole covered. The tone was good. High C.

Then I tried to do both tones in order. Low C, high C. Again. Until I got it right. And when I did I recognized a tune. Not "Swanee River," but the beginning of "Somewhere Over the Rainbow." I didn't know the third note, but I knew the first two. I was a musician. And I had my own instrument, bought with my own money. The M&Ms I would share with my sisters, but the ocarina was not a toy to be

new job?"

"It was OK. I made a little money." I took the twenty-four cents out of my pocket and held it up. "I bought M&Ms to share, and a surprise for next Sunday after dinner."

"Mommy, can we have some M&Ms now?" asked my sisters, looking with menace at the shiny brown bag which I held high out of their reach.

"No, they're for after supper. Daddy will be home in a minute, and then we'll eat."

In a corner of the living room was a large glass bottle that we used as a coin bank. Every Saturday night, my father would empty his pockets of loose change and put the coins in the bottle. The money would be used for summer vacation.

With an air of importance, I walked over to the bank and paused until I had the attention of the women, then took four pennies and a dime and began to drop them one by one through the slit. The first penny landed with a healthy ring on the other coins, but the second one missed and rolled behind the bottle. As I got down on all fours to retrieve the coin, I heard the screen door open and someone say, "Sshhh."

Standing with the errant penny in my hand I continued my grandiose gesture of giving to the family till. As I was depositing the dime, I turned to see my father standing in the doorway, my sisters in his arms. There was a pause. No one moved. Things had gone awry. This show was supposed to be for the women, my father's show would come the following Sunday. I would not show off money matters to my father. After all, I should be paying him back for the shoeshine kit first. Perhaps I should not have bought the ocarina but given all the money to him instead.

I stood there, embarrassed. The display should have ended with a hug from my mother, but now it was too complex.

"Sixty-five cents. I made sixty-five cents, sir."

I walked over to where he stood. He put my sisters down and squatted, so his eyes were level with mine. I reached in my pocket for the last dime and held it out to him.

"Where's the rest of it?"

"Fourteen cents in the bottle, five cents for M&Ms, and thirty-six cents for ... a surprise. Ten cents to help pay you back for the kit."

"A surprise?"

"Next Sunday after supper, I'll have a surprise for you. A music surprise."

He put his hand out. I put the dime in his hand. He looked at it, turned it over so the "heads" side was up.

"See the woman, son?"

I looked at the coin closely. Indeed, there was a woman's face. I'd never noticed that it was a woman before, I'd thought it was the pagan god Mercury, because of the wings like the FTD logo.

"Yes, sir."

"See what her name is?"

"Liberty?" Deep within me a wisecrack began to rise to the surface—*1950, her name is 1950*—but I did not dare make a crack now; my father was trying to teach me something.

I looked at the coin. I looked at my father, then at my mother. If she had shorter hair, and little wings coming out from the sides of her head...

"I think I'll save this dime, Dad," I said, pocketing it with my left hand and extending my right to shake his hand like the gentleman I was becoming. "And thanks for getting me started in business."

"Dinner, anyone?" said my mother. "Wash your hands, you kids."

My sisters flew up the stairs to the bathroom. I went into my room and opened the top drawer of my bureau. I took out a little box where I kept special stuff. Among the articles was a clear plastic pouch that held medals, mostly images of the Blessed Mother, rays of grace streaming from her hands. I dropped in the coin with Liberty, heads up. She fit right in. I got an inkling at that moment of how someone might come to worship money, since the only difference between the dime and the other objects in the pouch was stringability. The dime didn't go on a chain.

I snapped the pouch shut and placed it back in the box, which I placed in turn back in the drawer. Then I reached into my pocket and pulled out the ocarina and placed it next to the box. I closed the drawer. I looked at my hands. They were stained with black and tan and oxblood polish. I went into the empty bathroom and washed them almost clean, then went downstairs to eat my dinner and deliver my family a full report of my day. I kept the secret of the ocarina to myself until the following Sunday, when I played "Swanee River" with only two mistakes.

The Virtuous
Shamrock Grower

*S*ister Patrick Mary liked me, I think. She was our third-grade teacher, and by the time I came to her, I had gotten the school game down pretty well. Academically I was thriving, reading beyond my grade level, winning spelling bees left and right, memorizing catechism well. I was also learning classroom protocol. Always the first to pick up dropped chalk, helpful in cleaning after school, careful in my forms of address to teachers, I was a budding Christian Gentleman. (The only criticisms of my behavior the nuns offered had to do with my tendency to daydream, but they took this as a challenge to their skill, and I wouldn't really get in trouble over this until the upper grades.) Given these charming qualities and the proximity of my house to the school, I was a willing and able candidate for extracurricular activities, like the St. Patrick's Day play of that year.

And so it was that Sister Patrick Mary came to class one day in February, a wry smile on her face, and made an announcement.

"Children, this year, for the first time in the history of Holy Cross Parochial School, we are going to have a play to celebrate the Feast of St. Patrick on March seventeenth."

The news set the room abuzz. This would be the first play of any kind at the school. Who would be in it? Who would play St. Patrick? Were there parts for everyone?

Sister continued. "Everyone will be in the chorus." We all squirmed enthusiastically, still keeping silence. "There are also some speaking parts."

Hands went up, including my own. "Ssster, Ssster."

"Now put your hands down, and I'll tell you what the play is." She held up a green pamphlet. "It's called *The Virtuous Shamrock Grower.* Who knows what a shamrock is?"

"Ssster, Ssster." This was an easy question. We had been cutting shamrocks out of green construction paper since first grade.

"Yes, Mary Ann?"

"A shamrock is a three-leafed clover from Ireland."

"Very good, Mary Ann."

"Ssster," I hissed, with more information.

"Edward?"

"Sister, St. Patrick used the shamrock to teach the pagans of Ireland the truth of the Trinity—three leaves, one plant; three persons, one God." This was information I had only recently acquired from a book on the saints given to me by my grandmother.

"Very good, Edward."

Does this mean I get to play St. Patrick in the play? I asked silently.

"The play tells the story," Sister went on, "of a contest in Ireland to see who could grow the best shamrock for the Fair. There are three main contestants. Two of them are mean and dishonest and the third one is virtuous and wins."

No St. Patrick at all in the play, I thought. What a disappointment.

The reason I wanted to play the saint had to do with the sacramental cycle of third grade. The year before we had

In the 1950s the church hierarchy in the northeastern United States felt that a child was mature enough at age eight. The form of the rite included the renewal of baptismal vows to renounce Satan and all his pomp (which had been done on our behalf by our godparents years before), the presentation of the candidate to the Bishop by a sponsor (like any secret society worth its salt), the anointing of the forehead by His Excellency (reflecting the earlier anointing at baptism), a blow on the cheek (a sign of our willingness to die for the Faith as a Soldier of Christ), and the selection of a new name to mark one's rebirth as a committed Christian Catholic. My interest in the play was connected to my choice of a new name. In honor of my mother's Irish heritage, I was choosing Patrick.

A word about the blow on the cheek. We had learned at the beginning of the year that the church was divided into three groups: the Church Suffering, which included the Souls in Purgatory; the Church Triumphant, including the souls that had made it into Heaven; and the Church Militant, Christian souls on earth. The image of a militant Christianity went back to Constantine and the vision of the conquering cross in the sky above his soon-to-be Christian troops.

Now in the 1950s, the Communist threat had allowed American Catholicism to take a warlike tone. We were told that at any time Commie soldiers could burst in upon us and dare us to declare our faith under threat of death. Our monthly air raid drills, during which we would hide under our desks until the all-clear signal, were rituals that supported our fear of this godless enemy. If we could receive a blow on the cheek without flinching before the Bishop, we could stand up to an atheist with a gun, or an atomic bomb.

Patrick was a great symbol for the Church Militant. Service in the Armed Forces was part of the Americanization of Irish Catholics; just as St. Patrick had driven the snakes out of Ireland, the Irish Catholic SAC Bomber pilots would keep the Communist snakes from our soil.

"The name of the virtuous shamrock grower is Patrick," Sister Patrick Mary said now.

So there would be one in the play after all, I thought, and he would have a lot of lines to memorize. Hands shot up all over the room.

"You have a good memory, Edward, would you like to play this part?"

Would I? What a silly question. At first I was surprised by the offering. When I heard *"Go, Ed"* whispered by my classmates, I knew it was meant to be. My spelling bee prowess had made me a kind of champion, a logical representative to the rest of the school. The only other guy that could do it was Joe Wusinich, and he was patting me on the back in congratulations, so I had to say yes.

"Come up to the front, now, and stand here. Joseph Wusinich, would you like to play the mayor of the town?"

My classmates offered more cheers as Joe joined me.

"Now there is a part for a girl. Kathleen O'Connell?"

To cheers from the girls, Kathleen came to the front.

"The parts of the other shamrock growers don't have many lines," Sister said, "but they have to be able to be sneaky and mean."

Joe and I pointed to Jackie Woulfe. "Ssster, Jackie, Jackie." He was our First Friday companion and enjoyed a

friends stood with me. Now if only Walt Wiseley could get in.

"Walt Wiseley could do the other bad guy," Joe said, as if by telepathy. "He's pretty sneaky."

None of the other boys seemed interested, so the part went to Walt. The gang of four, plus Kathy O'Connell. This was going to be fun.

Sister Patrick Mary must have known what she was doing, choosing us boys. We all lived in Westbrook Park, except for Kathy, who wasn't too deep into the Springfield side of the parish to walk home after school. It felt a little unfair to me that the entire row by the window, by alphabetical chance and geographic fortune, had been emptied by her choices, but at least I'd be with my friends.

"Here are your scripts, children," Sister said. "Please memorize the lines in the first scene by next Tuesday. Now go back to your seats. Class, you are all in the chorus, and will sing a song at the end. Look at the side board."

On the blackboard were written the words to "When Irish Eyes Are Smiling." "Some of you may know the tune. Sing it with me if you do."

As the rest of the class sang, we in the cast started looking at our scripts. I did have a lot of lines, it was true, but I had no doubt that I could do the job. I had never been on a stage before, but I had been entertaining my extended family since I received a toy piano in the first grade. My first tune was "Swanee River," and it was a big hit. It had become our custom on holidays and some Sundays to have one of the children perform after dinner, so I knew I wouldn't have stage fright, but all those lines would take some work.

By the time Ed Sullivan came on the following Sunday, I had my lines in the first scene down. It was mostly composed of the mayor's announcement of the contest, some boasting by the shamrock growers ending in veiled threats by my competitors, and a conversation between the hero and the ingenue about how she would marry him only if he won the contest. Kathy O'Connell was all right for a girl. She was smart and kept her hair nice, but I was glad I didn't have to kiss her or anything.

Our first rehearsal went smoothly, though Jackie didn't have all of his six lines memorized and the rest of us had to cover for him without being too obvious. The part between Kathy and me was embarrassing, but my friends didn't make me crack up with any mouth noises, although they could have. We were beginning to be comrades in arts, understanding for the first time the phrase, "The play's the thing."

The second scene called for props, specifically three pots of shamrocks. Sister called on Ann Munday, who was artistic, to do the job and she did it well. The next Tuesday there were three small flower pots with several cardboard shamrocks on pencil stems.

In addition, Sister brought in two bottles with labels she had made showing a skull and crossbones and the word POISON written in shaky red letters. In this scene, when the other two contestants realize that they might lose if they play fair and square, they each plot separately to poison Patrick's plant. The last part of this scene had little dialogue but a good deal of skulking around on stage and, of course, mistaken pot identity, resulting in the evil being thwarted and turned back upon itself—the hero's plant is untouched, and the villains poison each other's plants.

Jackie and Walt were terrific in this scene, sneaking around the curtains, mugging to the imaginary audience.

The third and final scene was not as well written, although it did have interesting props—three larger flower pots, one with green shamrocks, belonging to the hero, of course, one with purple and one with brown plants, belonging to the auto-thwarted villains. The scene consisted of the presentation of the plants in the contest, the awarding of the prize, and a final speech by the hero extolling the virtues of Ireland, Irish colleens, and Irish Catholicism. Sister had added the song at the end.

My final speech was the hardest to learn. It was the first time I had ever heard the word *colleen*, and I didn't know exactly what it meant, but I did know that I was supposed to go to Kathleen O'Connell, who was sitting shyly on the stage, and help her to her feet and hold her hands with both of mine. The stage direction was so embarrassing and distracting that it took a long time to get it straight.

The dress rehearsal, the day before the production, went well, although I was envious of the villains' costumes—all black, with black capes to make the skulking even more outrageous. My own costume was regular school pants and shoes, regular shirt and tie, and a green vest with sparkles and shamrocks and a cellophane green hat. Kathleen had a green apron, but she was allowed to at least wear a party dress from home. The chorus wore their school clothes and whatever green accessory they could dig up. The Italian kids, as usual, outdressed the Irish.

The dress rehearsal was the first time the whole class got to see the show, and it was the first time anyone got to use the new risers, on which the chorus was to stand. My final speech was delivered almost without mistake, and the song was pretty good. The skulking scene was getting tighter and sharper. The next day we would do it before the whole school.

As I walked home from school with my co-stars after dress rehearsal, we discussed the last scene. I was concerned that it was a letdown after the antics of scene two.

"If only there was a way to jazz it up," I said, meaning, *If only I could steal the thunder back from you guys hamming it up with the skulking and the black capes.* The scene had gotten longer each time, and I suspected I was no longer the real hero, more lines or not.

"It's not that bad," said Joe, the mayor, and a more generous actor than myself. "And the song at the end will make it interesting for the little kids, anyway."

We reached my house first, and I said goodbye, leaving my friends to discuss the issue as they walked on.

The next day the class was electric. The chorus was even more greenly adorned than the day before. Right after the Pledge of Allegiance and prayers, we had a short Feast Day party for Sister. We gave her a clock for her desk, chosen by one of the parents, for which we chipped in twenty-five cents each. In fact, I think we gave a desk clock to every teacher up through eighth grade. Sister loved the clock—so she said—and the green-iced cake from Orlando's Bakery on Baltimore Pike.

As we were singing "Happy Feast Day to You," a note came up the aisle from Walt Wiseley. *Don't worry about the last scene,* it read. I turned around and got the OK sign from him and Jackie. I felt comforted and supported. How lucky ~~I was to have such good friends.~~

~~for reasons...~~

Jackie, Joe, and Walt were the last ones to leave the room. They should have been right behind me, but they weren't. I looked for support, but they were still in the classroom. I started back to see what was keeping them when they appeared, hurriedly closing the door behind them, walking quickly and somewhat stiffly to catch up.

"Sshh," I warned.

"It's gonna be great," whispered Jackie with a glint in his eye that I figured came from his imminent success. We caught up to the others and filed into the front rows of the seats for a pep talk from Sister.

"Now, boys and girls, I know you're nervous, but you're going to be just fine. Remember, the audience doesn't know the real play, so if a mistake is made, they won't know unless you let them know by laughing on stage. Whatever happens, just go right on with the play, and everybody will be fine.

"Now, here comes the rest of the school. Chorus, stay seated until the curtain closes after the second scene, then come backstage and take your place on the risers. Principals, go backstage now, the props are already back there. Break a leg, everybody."

Sister had told us the week before of St. Genesius, patron saint of actors, who had been a pagan mime in ancient Rome and whose act included making fun of the Christians' rite of Baptism, until one day the sacrament "took" and he became converted on stage, as it were. When he refused to finish the show on religious grounds, the Emperor and the rest of his audience thought it was part of the act. When he persisted in his refusal, he was ordered roped to a cross and his legs broken, resulting in his death by loss of blood. The phrase *Break a leg* was used, she told us, by actors all over the world in honor of his courage and artistic integrity. He, too, was a soldier of Christ. I wondered which was worse—having your legs broken or being turned to ashes in a bomb blast.

The five of us went backstage, joined in a moment by Sister. We could hear the sounds of the audience filling the seats out front. Tension was rising among us. The butterflies in my stomach had turned to sparrows, on their way to eagles. Jackie made a move toward the part in the curtain to look out. Sister stopped him cold.

"Touch that curtain, Mr. Woulfe, and you are out of the play."

The eighth-grader in charge of pulling the curtain came onstage with the news that all the classes were in the auditorium. He took his position stage right, and Sister called the five of us together in a circle.

"Now, whatever happens, just keep going," Sister repeated. "The audience won't know the difference. Let's offer the show up for the poor souls in Purgatory," she said, reminding us that we, as members of the Church Militant, could gain graces and early dismissal for the Church Suffering. We all blessed ourselves, and she went out to introduce the play and tell the audience what was expected of them. We heard her voice through the heavy curtain explaining good manners of the theater and encouraging their applause at the end.

We gave each other thumbs-up signals. Sister reappeared, and the eighth-grader opened the curtain.

The first scene went well. Nobody forgot any lines, we projected our voices to the confessional booths in back as we had been instructed, and we got applause as the curtain closed. It was my first taste of the sweet intoxicant that would influence my life ever after. I was proud of myself and

doing exactly, but I could tell the audience loved it. Jackie and Walt were grinning widely when the curtain closed.

The rest of our classmates began to appear backstage and take their places as townspeople on the risers. My two rivals disappeared into the dark corner of the stage and came back just as everyone had settled into position. When the curtain opened we heard an excited buzz from the audience—cries of recognition from the brothers and sisters of the chorus members. A few of the townspeople waved surreptitiously, and Mary Spellman nearly fell off the top riser.

The climax of the show came at the beginning of the third scene when the mayor calls the contestants onto the stage for the judging. I was to enter from the center, the other two from either side. The mayor would say a few words and put a medallion around my neck, and the villains would walk off.

The entrance happened as planned, though Jackie and Walt were both walking with a strange limp. *Another attempt to steal the show,* I thought to myself. *Why are they doing this to me?* The mayor said a few words about each of them getting their just desserts and was placing the medal— which was shaped as a shamrock and made of cardboard covered with tinfoil—around my neck when they both reached under their belts and drew out yardsticks from their pants legs.

As Jackie and Walt crossed swords, there were two reactions: a cheer from the audience, and a gasp of horror from the kids on the risers. What followed was a fight to rival Errol Flynn and Zorro put together. In their black clothes and capes, they took turns forcing each other against the wall on either side of the stage. As they neared the rest of us, Kathleen O'Connell jumped into my arms, but nobody noticed, and I did my best to shield her from the violence.

Third-graders began jumping off the risers. The girls were screaming; some of the boys were taking sides and shouting encouragement to the combatants. Soon the stage was cleared of everyone but the Zorros—and me and Kathleen, center stage, embracing. The swordsmen made their way downstage center. I heard Sister yelling to the eighth-grader, "Close it, close the curtain," but he was too busy watching the fight to obey. I was sure she was going to come out on stage and stop the show herself, thus breaking her own rules of stagecraft, but she didn't have to, because all of a sudden two yardsticks passed through the stomachs—actually under the upstage arms—of each villain, and groans of dying Irishmen filled the auditorium. They each went down on one knee, dropped their swords, still groaning, then fell flat on their faces and lay still for a second. They couldn't resist throwing in a few death throes, each not wanting the other to have the last word, and breathed their last, loudly and together.

Kathleen and I, just upstage of them, realized we were embracing, and separated. Sister's directive rang in my ears: *If a mistake is made, they won't know unless you let them know.* I called into the wings for the townspeople to return to the stage and take their places on the risers, the danger had passed. Then I took my new fiancé's hand and led her over the dead bodies to the front of the stage and gave my final speech, ending with a eulogy for my rivals.

"They were both good men. And they would have been great soldiers of Christ had they lived—their swordplay proved that. They would have kept the Communists of

Then we sang "When Irish Eyes Are Smiling," and the curtain closed.

The audience went wild. Jackie and Walt got up for the curtain call. We all took our bows. The applause for the duelists was deafening.

The curtain closed again. Girls from the chorus were hugging each other; a group had gathered around Kathleen. An icy voice commanded us to line up and march back to the classroom. It was like a recess bell had rung. We started back glumly. When we arrived there we took our seats, hands on our desks, and waited. Sister sat at her desk in the front of the room and glared. The new clock ticked loudly.

Finally she spoke. "Mr. Woulfe and Mr. Wiseley, come to the front of the class, please."

They obeyed.

"And bring the yardsticks with you."

They obeyed.

"Now put them back where they belong."

They obeyed, Jackie returning his to the side-board chalk ledge, Walt to the front-board ledge. They returned to the desk where Sister sat.

"Now face the class and tell them what you have to say."

Walt looked genuinely repentant, Jackie not at all, though his shoulders were drooped to Sister's satisfaction.

"I'm sorry," said Walt.

"I'm sorry," said Jackie, "but I'm glad we gave the virtuous shamrock seller, Ed Stivender, a chance to do what Sister said, just go right on, no matter what happens." Ever the rebel, ever the friend.

Sister's face was contorted with a mixture of anger and pleased surprise. My friends sat down. I turned around and gave Jackie a thumbs up.

"Someone could have been hurt."

But no one was, we all thought to ourselves.

"But no one was," she continued, perhaps reading our minds. "And part of the reason that no one was hurt might be related to the practice the two of you put in outside of normal rehearsal and school time." The two nodded. I breathed a sign of relief and amazement.

"Now if only you could see your way clear to pay as much attention and consideration to your schoolwork, perhaps you would both do much better, especially you, Mr. Woulfe."

"Yes, Sister," said Jackie, repentant but proud at this turn of events.

"And as for the rest of you, I'm proud of the job you did, and you won't have any homework tonight as a reward. Now we will sit quietly with our hands on the desks, folded."

Sister Patrick Mary sat down at her desk and raised a large picture book in front of her face. That part of her veil still visible above the book was shaking with silent laughter.

*T*he repertoire of the communication of love may well be infinite. Anthropologists have identified many types of courting behavior that seem aberrant to us but not to members of the culture from which they spring. In the fifth-grade culture of the Catholic elementary school in the 1950s, however, the grammar of love was rather limited. Kissing was out of the question, except in the highly formalized games of Spin the Bottle and Post Office played at Faith Maiocco's house at her questionable Friday night parties, to which I was invited only once.

If kissing was not allowed, petting was not even contemplated. Love scenes in the movies required the stars to have their feet on the bedroom floor, and television offered nothing more risqué than Jackie Gleason's "you're the greatest" chaste kiss at the end of a "Honeymooners" episode.

Written expressions of love were frowned upon—as were all passed notes—except at Valentine's Day when a card was more a political act of voting for the most popular kids in the class than a message of real affection.

There was really only one option in 1957, in the Archdiocese of Philadelphia, if a parochial school boy wanted to show his love to a parochial school girl: he would steal her hat from her head in the schoolyard and hope that she cared enough about him to chase him and "try"—never very hard—to get it back. Success in retrieval would be a great put-down, even worse than ignoring that it had been taken. Standing with hands on hips, feigning anger, was somewhere in the middle, and the expression on the victim's face would have to be read carefully for the exegesis of the text.

What made the hat game possible was, in part, the fact that Catholic girls wore hats year-round—to church, especially, but also to school, summer and winter, in case the student body was called to Mass. Thanks to St. Paul, and a comment in one of his epistles, women and girls had to be covered in church so as not to tempt angels. So hats were important and abundant. (If a woman was caught off guard without a hat on her way to Mass there were some Jesuitical solutions available, the bottom line of which was a paper tissue bobby-pinned in place.) After Vatican II, this rule was rescinded and hats disappeared, except in winter and at Easter. I have no idea what a ten-year-old boy does nowadays.

Nor do I know how many times I stole Diane Tasca's hat that year; I do know that I never passed it to a confederate nor threw it in the trash or on the roof of the school, and I always returned it before the recess bell rang. And I also know that I loved her—as deeply as a ten-year-old boy could.

Of course, I had been infatuated before. In first grade there was a bicameral desire for the Ronan twins, Gloria and Patricia. In fourth grade I spent some time mooning over a postulant named Sister Mary Rebecca. Since she had not taken her final vows, her headdress was less constrictive than that of the older nuns, and a brown wisp of hair always peeked out, inviting me to wonder bout the rest of her. She had once asked me why I always looked so grave. I mistook the word to mean "fixing to die," so I never declared my love openly, but found some solace in knowing I would meet her again in Heaven.

~~M h f D~~ ~~Diane Tasca was~~ different—it was real. It

~~Pep is a~~

sometimes see in the supporting actresses in surfing movies—a mixture of positive attitude and *joie de vivre*. You could see it in the way she held herself—chin up, grinning, facing forward, plowing through the moment, her hair like Little Lulu in the Sunday comics. You can still see it in the class picture from that year—her hands on the desk, not simply folded like the rest of us, but thrust there with purpose and will, her face looking directly at the camera, her eyes full of the light of the moment. Pep.

It was her pep that lent energy to her response to my hat theft. Invariably hands would go to hips, waist would bend slightly, and she would say—never shriek or cry—but say loudly, "Edward, give me back my hat," followed by a few vain attempts to get it back, never strong or peppy enough to be successful. That would have ruined it.

This was no common game of keepaway, which was also played in the same schoolyard. The major factor that distinguished it was my technique of keeping the hat to myself and not passing it to another boy, as would have been proper in keepaway played well. This would have been a breach of trust, a cheapening of our implicit bond. In taunting someone else such a move would have been appropriate, but not in this case. This was private. This was love—or something like it.

One day there was an incident with the hat of Kathleen Harper, a somewhat slower girl in the class who sometimes drooled on her uniform. We had tolerated her at lesser or greater degrees and kept our teasing to a minimum. At recess, however, on the first nice day of spring, she was watching some of the other girls jump rope when her hat disappeared from her head. She wheeled around and saw Billy Bacciagalupe waving it around tauntingly. She lunged for the hat but was no match for Billy and some of the other sixth-grade boys who had joined him. They now began to toss it back and forth among themselves. Kathleen was as good a sport as she could be and was going through the motions of response to this injustice, almost running to get it back.

Watching the scene from the doorway, I looked around for a nun, but there was none in sight. And so I joined the fray, betraying my sex for the first time in an attempt to stop unfair play. The hat was flying in midair between Billy and George Lauer when I jumped up and brought it down.

"Yo, Ed, throw it here," came voices from either side. Ignoring them, I returned the hat to a teary-eyed, drooling Kathleen, though I heard groans from the sixth-grade boys. Out of the corner of my eye I saw Diane watching me.

"Whatsamatter, Eddie, playing with the girls? ... Eddie and Kathleen sitting in a tree / k-i-s-s-i-n-g / first comes love, then comes marriage / then comes a baby in a baby carriage."

Now they were surrounding me menacingly, and still there was no nun in sight.

"Time for a visit to the spit pit."

The spit pit was a stairwell to the basement of the annex, around the corner and out of sight of the rest of the yard. The railings at the top made perfect perching places for the spitters to get English on the hostage unlucky enough to be thrown down the steps. I was being jostled by the bigger boys in that direction. Still no nuns. I was doomed.

As I reached the bottom of the stairs, a miracle occurred. The recess bell rang, freezing even Billy Bacciagalupe in his tracks. I looked up from my place of ignominy to see

gone.

I ran as fast as I could to catch up to my class, but I was late and arrived at the door of the classroom after it had been shut. I tried to sneak in but Sister Regina Christi caught me.

"Edward, do you have a good excuse for your lateness?"

"No, Sister, no excuse." I shot a look at Diane. Her face was full of understanding, I thought. To report how I had rescued Kathleen Harper would have cheapened the event, and to rat on boys from another class would have broken another of the complex codes of suburban boyhood.

"I'm surprised at you, Edward. You'll stay after school today and sweep the floor."

"Yes, Sister." This wasn't a real punishment for me. It would let me play near the incinerator when it was trash time. It was my favorite—a roaring, contained fire like the hellish scene in Ming's dungeon on "Flash Gordon." Throwing trash into it slowly was a great treat.

I sat down and put my attention in my copy book. Sister started a catechism drill.

When I looked up from my copy book, a folded piece of paper appeared on my desk. It was torn out of a memo pad and had been drooled upon. I opened it. Scrawled on it were the words *Thank you.* I looked over at Kathleen and smiled and blinked my eyes. She smiled and blinked her eyes and drooled.

That afternoon, after I had swept the floor and emptied the pencil sharpener, I took the trash in a paper bag out to the incinerator, my books in hand. This way I could stay out there watching the fire as long as I wanted.

"Good afternoon, Sister. It won't happen again," I prophesied.

"Very good, Edward. Be careful with the fire."

When I got out back the furnace was roaring, the waxen milk and orange juice cartons from lunchtime feeding the gold-vermillion dragon. Student helpers were not expected to put anything into the fire itself but to simply leave the trash by the side of the brick oven. First I threw in the crumpled papers, then lower down the waxed papers from the kids who ate their lunch in the room because they lived too far to walk home for lunch, and finally the sawdust from the pencil sharpeners. If thrown correctly, the dust would incinerate before it fell. It did.

My science and punishment finished, I started home. The day was beautiful. As I was passing the convent, out the door came Diane, fresh from her piano lesson. I stood at the end of the path and waited for her. She grinned when she saw me.

"Finished your punishment?"

"Yeah, it was easy. Been watching the fire." It occurred to me that I could have been seen as dawdling, waiting for her, but that wasn't it at all, honest.

"Walk you home?" I asked, surprising myself.

"It's out of your way, though."

"I got time."

As we walked down Springfield Road toward her house and away from mine she said, "I saw what you did for Kathleen today."

"I didn't do anything for Kathleen," I said defensively. "I did it for myself." It was beginning to dawn on me that what I had done could be construed as a betrayal of Diane.

"What do you mean?"

"When I see somebody helpless being picked on I feel

well." She lived on the other side of the development. I only saw her at church or school.

"Do you like me?"

"Oh, yes, I really like you, Diane," I blurted back, resisting the desire to throw myself at her feet and hold her knees.

"Then why do you steal my hat?"

I was flabbergasted. Diane Tasca, girl of my dreams, thinking that I was as mean as Billy Bacciagalupe.

"Be—be—*because* I like you so much."

"Then Billy likes Kathleen, I guess."

Now I was getting in deeper and deeper.

"No, he hates her. He's afraid of her, probably, afraid he'll catch her retardedness or something."

"So, you steal my hat because you hate me."

"No, it's the opposite."

"Then what's the difference?" Her pep was turning to pout, not unattractively, I thought, but still...

"For one thing, I'm not afraid of you—catching your retardedness, I mean. I mean, you're not retarded, you're real smart."

"Afraid of catching my smartness?"

"I'd love to catch your smartness..." I was foundering in a rising tide of adrenalin and hormones, my mind racing to get ahead of her next question, but I didn't know where it would come from. "Wait, look, if I didn't like you I'd steal your hat and throw it to Jackie Woulfe or Walt Wiseley, but I don't. I keep it myself."

"Then you're selfish and don't want to share."

"Share your hat? No."

"Then you want to keep it all to yourself?"

"I give it back to you, don't I?" There.

"Yes, but it's still ungentlemanly."

"Do you want me not to do it anymore?"

She stopped walking midway through my question. I stopped and turned around to face her.

"Well, yes and no," she replied, her eyes looking up as though she were solving a difficult math problem.

"Yes and no?" Now I felt like a helpless student with a tutor who knew much more than I about the subject. It was the first time I had come up against a feminine mind with deeper wisdom. It would not be the last.

"No, I don't want you to stop because I like the attention you give me when you do it. In a weird way it makes me feel appreciated."

I was almost getting it, but not quite. "And yes?"

"Yes, I want you to stop because it interferes, the attention I mean, with my vocation, and yours as well, I think."

If I had been skilled in the arts and sciences of Love I surely would have blurted out, *But I don't have a vocation.* However, this possibility had been with me since baptism.

The word *vocation* can refer to any of the answers to the question, "What do you want to be when you grow up?" But in our tradition it meant one thing—being called to devote your life to God as a priest (or a brother if you didn't have the test scores to be a priest) if you were a boy or being called to be a nun if you were a girl.

The word has its roots in the Latin *vocare*—to call—and since first grade it had been drilled into us that some of us ̶ ̶ ̶ ̶ ̶ ̶ ̶ ̶ ̶ ̶ ̶ by God to serve Him in a special way.

̶ ̶ ̶ ̶ ̶ ̶ ̶ ̶ ̶

threat to the vocation. If one had a vocation and did not respond to it, there was a place in the darkest region of Hell for you.

There was a picture in the catechism of a young man standing at a three-path crossroads trying to decide which way to go. A road leading up the hill toward heavenly light was marked *Religious Life*, a road leading ambiguously straight was marked *Family Life*, a road leading downward into storms was marked *Single Life*. The lesson was clear— single life without religious service would be dreadful; married life could go either way; priesthood was the best.

As I stood there on Springfield Road, I felt like a fool. Apparently my tutor had done a lot more thinking about this than I. I needed to counter with an argument. I chose *reductio ad adsurdum*.

"In other words it would be better if I was like Billy, stealing your hat to be mean."

Diane began to walk again.

"Not better, but easier, I think."

"For who?"

"For both of us."

"Do you really think you have a vocation?" I asked.

"Well, I haven't heard any voices, but I have thought about it a lot. How about you?"

"My mother really wants me to be a priest, but my father has warned me against taking a job where I have to wear a dress to work."

Diane looked at me, her cheeks reddening from the shock of my answer. I couldn't keep a straight face. We both started laughing.

"Edward Patrick Stivender, you're twisted," she said, using the term that was just beginning to gain popularity. Then with an action efficient as it was quick she took my baseball cap from my head and raced down the street. By the time I recovered from the surprise she was a few yards from her door. When I caught up to her she was at her door, grinning triumphantly, my cap twirling on her finger.

"Never get a job where you have to wear a hat to work," she giggled as she threw it back to me. She disappeared into the house, leaving a confused and winded fifth-grade boy to figure out the meaning of the moment.

As I walked back down Springfield Road I tried to imagine the possibilities open to us. What if we both followed our vocations? Maybe we could serve in the same parish, Diane as principal of the school, me as pastor. We wouldn't be able to hug or kiss, but that wasn't the most important thing in a love as fine as ours. What if Diane went in the convent and I stayed in the single life? Then I could be a kind of single knight, like Galahad, pure but committed to his Lady who was out of reach. What if I took Holy Orders and she stayed single? No, she would surely get married to someone else. Maybe I could marry them to each other. What a gallant priest I'd be. But I wasn't sure I had a vocation. There was still time to figure all this out, wasn't there?

A few weeks later Sister Regina Christi told the class that Diane had an announcement. As she rose from her seat and started to the front of the room I tried to guess what the news was. Was she going into the convent already? Although this ~~would have been~~ extraordinary it was not unheard of. At her

Pittsburgh," she said. "We will join him this weekend." And then she sat down.

Moving? I thought to myself. *She's moving away?* I felt the same mixture of loss and betrayal as I had when my sister had knocked a newly completed model bi-plane out of my hand and sent it crashing to the floor where it broke in two. But I did not cry, as I had then. I stared at her. She put her head on the desk. A few of the kids around her were patting her on the back to try to make her feel better.

Sister spoke. "We will have a goodbye party on Friday afternoon right after the tic-tac-toe game. Now open your spelling books to page fifty-eight."

Diane was absent for the rest of the week—helping the family pack, I figured. When she returned on Friday she was surrounded by girlfriends in the recess yard and at lunch, so I didn't have a chance to speak to her, though I'm not sure what I would have said. Meanwhile I was trying to discern if this was a sign from above that I had a vocation.

As fate would have it, the contestants of this week's game were myself and Diane. It was the culmination of a series in which we had each defeated a number of opponents in our version of a popular TV quiz game, "Tic Tac Dough," which tested the players' fund of knowledge. The game began when Sister asked Mike Menseck to go to the board and draw the four lines that produced the nine squares that each represented a different subject.

A coin toss would determine which contestant would go first. Diane and I took our places in the front of the room, and Sister flipped the coin.

"Heads," said Diane. The coin hit the floor and spun, then flattened.

"Tails," said Sister. "Edward, you win the toss."

Although I wanted to win the game, I also wanted to be a gentleman and make a gesture of affection to the girl of my dreams. I had, after all, been afraid to steal her hat since our talk. So I said, "I defer to Diane, Sister. She may go first."

Diane understood my sign, I think, because she smiled at me.

"Top right square, Sister, please."

"The category is Geography. The question is 'What is the major export of Texas?'"

Without pausing, Diane answered, "Crude oil." It was the only crude thing I ever heard her say.

"Correct. Edward?"

"Middle square, please, Sister."

"Arithmetic. How much is eleven squared?"

My mind's eye roved to the multiplication table in the back of the copy book to the space catty-corner to the final one (144), and I spoke. "One hundred and twenty-one."

A whispered roar went up from the boys.

"Correct. Diane?"

"Lower right-hand corner."

"The category is Spelling. The word is 'encyclopedia.'"

This produced a groan from the boys. This was an easy one since even the slowest person in class knew Jiminy Cricket's song from "The Mickey Mouse Show" with the spelling of the word in the chorus.

"E-n-c-y-c-l-o-p-e-d-i-a." Diane almost chanted.

The girls fidgeted enthusiastically.

"Correct. Edward?"

"Middle left square, please."

Joe Wusinich shot me look of consternation. Middle left would leave her a space to win. I couldn't explain to him in

Would that it were so, I thought. Would that it were ever so.

"The category is Civics. How many seats in the United States Senate?"

Easy, two from each state. "Ninety-six." High signs from the boys.

"Correct. Diane?"

"Middle right square, please."

"This is for the win. Quiet, please. Name the Seven Sacraments."

A groan from the boys. Joe Wusinich put his head down on the desk. This was too easy. Second-grade stuff. Every girl was grinning.

"Baptism, Penance, Holy Eucharist, Confirmation, Holy Orders, Extreme Unction..." Then she paused. We all held our breath. She had skipped Matrimony. Could it be that she forgot? Forget Matrimony, culmination of even a Barbie Doll's dream?

Diane looked at me and then, in a firm loud voice that was beyond pep, said, "Taking the vows of a nun: poverty, chastity, and obedience."

A groan from the girls, a cheer from the boys. Sister's face was flushed, her mouth open in surprise.

"Wrong. Edward, name the Seven Sacraments."

I looked down the row where I sat, all the boys had their fingers crossed, some had their eyes closed, as if in prayer.

"The Seven Sacraments are Baptism, Penance, Holy Eucharist, Confirmation, Holy Orders, Extree Munction"—this is how it was popularly pronounced, the general public knew it as "last rites"—"and *Matrimony.*"

The boys were cheering, straining out of their desks. The girls looked sad; Kathleen was drooling and crying. But Diane was grinning from ear to ear as she crossed in front of Sister's desk toward me, her hand extended.

"Congratulations, Edward."

I took her hand. "Thanks, Diane." I was about to say something about wanting her to win when the class started singing, and in the door came Cherie Armao and Cathy Consalvi carrying a cake with *Good Luck in Pittsburgh* written on it in blue and cerise letters.

We all sang "For She's a Jolly Good Classmate" and lined up for a piece of cake. The bell rang to end the school day before the cake was finished. I waited around until the walkers, riders, and bus kids filed out. Diane was cleaning out her desk, returning her books to a box in the closet. They were all in perfect condition, wrapped in brown paper, the soft covers supported by inserted thin cardboard.

"Can I help carry your books home?" I asked. I felt a little silly waiting for her.

"No books to carry," she laughed. "You can carry my hat if you want."

She held out the winter hat that she had left months before in her locker. It was the easiest to steal, a tam with a yarn clump at the top—a perfect handle. I took it and put it in my army-style bookbag.

Diane went to Sister to say goodbye. The nun hugged her hard, her starched bib made a cracking sound. They were both crying. I looked away.

"I want you to have this rosary, Diane. It was blessed by the Pope."

corridor to the principal's office and waited outside. When she came out her eyes were red and her nose was running. I pulled a clean and—thanks, Mom—ironed handkerchief out of my back pocket and handed it to her. She used it and kept it in her hand as we walked down Springfield Road toward her house. My mind was racing, torn between having to say goodbye and the confusion I felt from winning the quiz game. Did she really forget Matrimony? Did she really think becoming a nun was a sacrament? Would I really never see her again?

"When do you leave?" I asked lamely.

"I'm all packed. If the movers are finished we leave this afternoon."

I looked down the street to see a large van blocking one lane of traffic. No one was carrying anything out to it. A couple of workers were leaning against it, smoking. We continued our walk silently. There was a question on the tip of my tongue but I was having trouble getting it out. This often happened with my father when I needed to ask for something. In that case I would take a deep breath and blurt it out. Now I was taking deep breaths, but nothing was coming.

"Are you all right?" she asked.

"Huh, sure, fine, I was just wondering, do you think becoming a nun is really more of a sacrament than Matrimony?" This question was overloaded with subtexts, though I didn't know it at the time.

We had almost reached her house. She began to answer but stopped at the sound of a loud bang coming from the van. We both looked quickly at the source of the noise. A worker had slammed the door into place and was sealing the lock with wire. Diane's mother was writing something on a clipboard. She looked up and saw us.

"Come on, Diane, we're almost ready," she said, and disappeared into the house.

"I have to go, Edward," she said. Then she kissed me, full on the lips. I was shocked by this gesture and took a step back. She ran up the sidewalk and into her house. The cab doors slammed.

"I love you," I called into the roar of the moving van engine as it started up.

I started walking back down the street, trying to figure out what her answer might have been and why she had given the answer she had to the quiz question. The thought that she had a vocation to become a priest tried to enter the internal forum of my ruminations, but it could not get through the door barred by the iron pole of canon law. Perhaps she really did have a vocation to the convent and it was her way of telling me that our love could never be—no matrimony for us.

And then it hit me. She had thrown the game and let me win! She did love me, or something like it. I took my bookbag and threw it into the air with elation. In midair her hat slipped out and fell at my feet. I picked it up, slung my bookbag over my shoulder, and started running back to her house. As I approached it I saw that the van was gone and her family's station wagon was not in the driveway.

I ran to the door and knocked loudly. The sound echoed back. I peeked in the front window and looked into an empty house, light slanting on bare woodwork. They were gone. I'd never see her again. I held the hat to my nose and breathed in the warm scent of her brown hair. I hung the hat on the

I've never seen my "permanent record," but I know it exists somewhere. On it are listed all my final grades for courses right through high school, as well as certain kinds of reprimands for evil deeds done, or required deeds omitted. A glance at it would yield some information about my performance in fifth grade. It was the first year I did not receive a medal for Religion or General Excellence. It was the first year I received a certificate for Perfect Attendance. I had gone to school every day, even when I could have stayed home sick, or pretending to be sick. School had become interesting. Life had become interesting. And there were two reasons—girls and Latin.

It was the year I fell in love with Diane Tasca. It was the year I won my first dance contest. It was the year I became an altar boy.

The dance contest was the easiest of the three. One day, while standing in line at the public school to receive my polio sugar cube, I noticed a sign announcing dance classes for boys and girls, fifth grade and up. I signed up and went every Saturday afternoon for five weeks, learning the fox-trot, the box step, the jitterbug, and the waltz. On the sixth Saturday there was a contest, and Mary Shillington and I won first prize for jitterbug. I was very proud of myself, as were my parents, whose living room dancing had inspired me.

It wasn't my dancing, however, that qualified me for the elite corps of boys chosen to assist the priest at God's altar during Mass. It was my reputation for being a quick study and, I found out later, the fact that I lived three doors from the church property.

First a word about the Catholic church in 1957. It may as well have been 1599, liturgically speaking. And that was fine with me. The altar was placed at the front of the church, or in our case, the all-purpose church hall. The priest spent much of his time with his back to the congregation. Much of what he said was inaudible to the people attending: some of it was whispered, especially the words at the Consecration of the Bread and Wine, and all of it was in Latin.

The Mass had not changed in form since the Counter-Reformation, specifically the Council of Trent, when the Vatican, in response to the paradigm shift in Europe known now as the Protestant Reformation, standardized its central act of worship into a form that would be the touchstone of some of the most beautiful music the West has ever known. Ironically the language of the Mass, once the common tongue of the people, had become a stumbling block by the twentieth century, when so few American Catholics spoke Latin that special individuals were chosen to speak for the people when responses to the prayers were necessary.

Later I would learn other names for this role—server, acolyte—but we called them altar boys. At the beginning of fifth grade a dozen of us were chosen to meet with Father Gatens after school. Each of us was given a little red booklet on the cover of which was a woodcut of a priest and two altar boys before an altar. Inside were the Latin responses as well as the movements mapped out in dotted lines. Each week we were to memorize a series of passages, and we were drilled by our teacher, Sister Regina Christi, in special sessions after school. Once we got going on the Latin, she turned us back over to Father Gatens for the rest of our training. He would show us how to handle the water and wine, the communion plate, the candles.

were put on a schedule of

combed my hair, and was

suddenly stopped before paste hit bristle. Brushing my teeth was too dangerous today. It could break the fast I had started at midnight out of respect for the reception of the Body of Christ at communion time. If one iota (the smallest unit of anything in the Catholic tradition, be it solid, liquid, verbal, or alphabetical) of the sugar that gives commercial toothpaste its fresh minty taste should happen to slide down my throat into my stomach, my fast would be ruined, and I would not be able to receive communion. At my first service of Mass. I would be a scandal. The only reason a person in 1957 did not receive communion, besides breaking of the fast, was that he had either been excommunicated or had committed a Mortal Sin without going to Confession. The only Mortal Sin likely to be available to a fifth-grade boy was touching himself.

Whew. Close call. I opened the medicine chest and powdered the bristles with bicarbonate of soda, which has no food content, and brushed.

Back in my room I dressed, all except for my shirt and tie. I knew there would be a starched and ironed white shirt waiting downstairs. I grabbed a clip-on tie from my closet and headed down the stairs, where my mother had just finished ironing. A stiff shirt and folded white handkerchief were waiting. I finished dressing, kissed her on the cheek, and flew out the door, *ad altare Dei*—"toward the altar of God, who gives joy to my youth." The opening line of the Mass.

Although the beginning of the church property was only three doors across the street from my house, the building to which I was going was another two hundred yards up the hill. By the time I got there, I was breathless. I slipped through the door, through the priest's sacristy, and down a hall to the altar boys' room. John Wood, smartest boy in sixth grade and an experienced server, was filling the cruets with cold water and cold Tokay altar wine from the refrigerator.

"I'm not nervous at all!" I blurted.

"Good thing," John chuckled. "I'd hate to see you drop the book."

The book! The largest book any of us had ever seen— the Missale Romanum, the extra large Latin Missal that graced the altar and had to be moved during the first part of the Mass. Later, when I heard about a judge "throwing the book" at a criminal I knew what book it was and how much it would hurt, and how strong judges must be to throw it. Not only was the book very large and heavy, it was ensconced on a large and heavy, though necessarily portable, oaken lectern. This lectern's holding surface was hinged so it could be adjusted by the priest to suit his eyesight or spectacle prescription; a metal wire rod in the back was placed into grooves in the oaken base.

There were two basic jobs for altar boys in those days— one would have the book, the other the bells—just one bell, actually, a hand-held bronze bell the ringing of which would signal the faithful to stand, kneel, sit, and so forth. Although "the book" was heavier, "the bells" were more important. A mistake in this arena would have the congregation sitting or kneeling at the wrong times, and the Mass might not count. So John, the more experienced of us, would take the bells.

As John went to deliver the cruets and basin to the credence table next to the altar, I approached the racks of surplices and cassocks. The cassock is a long red robe with

surplice.

The surplice is a white garment not unlike the top of "baby doll" pajamas (as I would discover years later when I started dating Protestant girls). An oversized blouse, it goes over the cassock. The problem in choosing one was not so much size as color. It is supposed to be white. The ones on the rack were variations of that color. Some were in fact white but with stained with wine or wax. Many were off-white, some gray, some beige from age or abuse. I chose the one in best condition and slipped it over my head, being careful not to muss my Wild Root Cream Oiled hair.

John returned with the "lightning rod." This was our nickname for an instrument used to light and extinguish candles set too high on the altar to reach with a simple match. Out of a wooden pole there rose two brass rods, one with a bell-shaped extinguisher, the other hollowed to hold a long waxen wick connected to a peg which could be used to adjust the length of the exposed wick. With a push of this peg a small light could be turned into a flaming torch, useful for scaring the fifth-grade girls.

John was holding the instrument as a drill sergeant on TV would hold a rifle. "Ready for this?" he grinned, honoring me with his trust. I held the rod, adjusted the wick while he lit it, then I started toward the altar, guarding the light with my cupped left hand while holding it like a crusaders' lance with my right. Of course it didn't go out, my name meant "Guardian of Light," after all.

I genuflected at the foot of the stairs leading to the altar, walked up one, two, three steps to the right, lit one, two, three tall candles on the altar, walked down one, two, three steps, genuflected, walked up one, two, three steps to the left, lit one, two, three tall candles, walked back down one, two, three steps, genuflected, and exited stage right. Out of the corner of my eye I saw a familiar face in the front row of collapsible chairs that served for a pew—my mother. The pressure was on.

In a sense, this was the start of my mother's dream come true. She wanted me to be a priest, and this was the first step. When one was the eldest son of an Irish Catholic woman, priesthood could serve as a way of redeeming one's family, getting someone on the inside who could represent the rest at the Last Judgment. It was also the highest role in the patriarchal society that Catholic Life is. If I succeeded here, I would be on my way.

I placed the lightning rod back on its hook in the wings and joined my partner in the priest's sacristy just as Father Gatens arrived, lending his scent of Old Spice and shoe polish to the rich tones of incense and extinguished beeswax wick. The smell of the "backstage" of a Catholic church, even a part-time church such as we had, is a rich smell indeed, well known to former altar boys all over the world. Even now a visit there evokes warm memories.

Father took off his coat and put on his alb, the white cassock reminding us of our baptism, while he said, in Latin, the prayers of preparation, reading from a card on the dressing table on which had also been placed the several vestments he would wear during this sacred rite. These prayers were meant to focus the priest's mind on the task to come. He put on the amice—a linen shawl—the stole, a large and fancy strip of cloth, sign of his priestly power, and then he held his hands behind his back, waiting for one of us to place in them the cincture, the woven rope that would be used as a belt.

I looked at John and he nodded, signalling me to step

reminiscent of the towel Christ used to wipe his disciples' feet at the Last Supper, to his sleeve, and steadied himself for the final garment, the chasuble. Made of green moire satin with a white cross embroidered with gold and silver thread, this final garment had been gently set by the altar nun the night before in three or four folds.

The next moment was a wonder to behold. Father took the corners of the garment between the thumb and forefinger of each hand, and with a flick of the wrist sent the thing flying into the air in such a way that it landed squarely on his shoulders, perfectly balanced, front and back. Father Gatens was the best. He took the chalice, covered with the same cloth as the chasuble, and turned and faced us. "Ready, boys." Six-thirty on the dot.

John and I preceded the celebrant out to the altar, took our places on either side of him and began the prayers at the foot of the altar, reciting in Latin the forty-second psalm. *"Introibo ad altare dei,"* intoned the priest.

"Ad Deum qui laetificat juventutum meum," we responded, speaking formally for the congregation. "I will go unto the altar of God, To God who brings joy to my youth."

Then we knelt for the first long prayer of the Mass, the "Confiteor," and as we did so, John and I reached behind us and flicked our cassocks off our heels. I got lost in the middle of the second line, but luckily at the center of the prayer there was a breast-beating part—"*mea culpa, mea culpa, mea maxima culpa* (through my fault, through my most grievous fault)"—so I caught up to my partner at that point and beat him to the end by a quarter of a second. I was cooking now.

And then it was time to move the book. I moved around to the left side of the altar and stood silently while Father read the epistle. When he had finished he moved to the center of the altar and waited for me. I walked up the one, two, three steps, braced myself, stood on tiptoe leaning against the altar cloth, and grabbed the lectern by the surface that held the book rather than by the base. I heard a gasp coming from the front row and a groan directly behind me. Not hearing these sounds as cues to coming disaster, I pulled the thing toward me, edging it off the altar. When the base did finally leave the altar it swung down and caught me in the stomach, causing me to stumble backwards down one, two, three steps and knocking the wind out of me in the bargain. Luckily, I recovered with a genuflection and stayed there for a moment regaining my balance, breath, and composure, the base swinging gently against my surplice. All I had to do now was walk up one, two, three steps and put the contraption back on the altar.

As I started my climb I could feel the loosened hem of the cassock cozying around my heel in such a way that when I started to walk I was walking inside the cassock. With a final burst of energy, I kicked through the buttons of the cassock and lunged toward the altar with my burden. The whole paraphernalia reached the altar and kept going, disappearing off the other side, taking two of the three candles with it. I myself did a clumsy *tour jete* and landed on my feet, three steps down to the side.

Father Gatens was standing calmly at the middle of the altar, his hands held out in priestly form. Slowly his head turned and he looked at me. "I had heard you were a dancer, Mr. Stivender, but is this really the time for it?" Sheepishly, I replaced the stand on the altar, placed the book on the stand,

mother never mentioned it to my sisters, so there was no memorial teasing. The rest of the congregation, their minds on the Rosary or their daily missals, probably didn't notice. And it wasn't until years later, when I was in college, that I understood how King David must have felt when he danced before the Ark of the Covenant.

One of the great things about tne design ~. ~....
families is cousins, especially cousins your age. You
can never have a brother your own age unless he is a twin,
and that brings its own set of problems, but a cousin comes
without those complications. My mother and her sister each
gave birth to her firstborn child within three months of each
other, both boys—me and my cousin Jimmy Beal. The
following year brought them each a girl, my sister Nancy
and Patty Beal. As we grew, this foursome became a political
force that exercised the lobbying power of the N.R.A. concerning decisions about vacations and holidays.

The Beals lived across the Delaware River in New
Jersey, in a suburb of Camden called Runnemede. Driving
time between the two homes, once the Walt Whitman bridge
was built, was less than an hour—not so far that a round trip
for Sunday dinner was unthinkable, but far enough that
sleeping over was an adventure for the children and a respite
for one set of parents.

Across the street from the Beals' house lived a family of
fundamentalist Christians. The father of the household was
tall and thin with deep-set eyes, almost a caricature of a fire
and brimstone preacher of another century. The only time

we really saw him was when he changed the signs in front of the house. These signs, made from old doors mostly, bore scriptural quotes and exhortations. They were backed up with radio broadcasts played loudly from the windows of the front porch. Although we were never sure of the number, there were several children living in the house as well as a pale wife. One of the children, as pale as her mother, was a girl about our age whose face we sometimes saw peeking behind the curtains of an upstairs window. If we waved or acknowledged her in any way, the face would disappear.

Down the side of their house, from the sidewalk into the backyard, grew a wildly healthy privet hedge which was the object of our favorite after-supper sport. We would start running from about twenty yards up the street and throw ourselves into it, spinning so that we hit the giant shrubbery with our back. It was like a great pillow that caught us, bent under our weight, and then lightly snapped back, depositing us on our feet. For all the times we did it, the hedge showed little damage.

For some reason, the father never tried to stop us. The household must have known we were doing it, because it was during this game that we saw the girl's face at the window. She looked so lonely that we decided she must be held there against her will. We began to plan all sorts of schemes to save her from her awful father. Prepubescent Princes Charming, armed with Uncle Tom's ladder, we plotted midnight raids and ambuscades, always talking ourselves out of these schemes for practical reasons. One day, though, we saw our chance.

The three of us—Jimmy, Tommy (his younger brother), and I—were playing chew-the-peg on the front lawn when she came around from back of her house with her bike. When she reached the street she hopped on and rode up the hill. We looked at each other in amazement. It was the first time we'd seen her outside the house or yard.

"Let's catch up and talk to her," said Jimmy. In a moment the three of us were in pursuit, finally coming alongside her as she turned the corner of the big block, out of sight of her house.

"Hold on. We just want to talk to you," I shouted, out

"Yes, we are," I piped up, hoping she wasn't a Communist spy prepared to kill us for our faith.

"Then you're strangers. My daddy says nothin' in the world stranger'n a Catholic. He says you worship statues and don't read the Bible."

"We do not worship statues. We worship what the statue represents," I said, proud of my catechetical knowledge and the fact that I got to use it doing the thing the catechism was invented for, debating with Protestants.

"Including Mary?" she shot back, laying a trap.

"Including Mary," said Jimmy, taking the bait.

"Well, Mary ain't no savior of mine, and it's vain to worship her. See, Catholics are strangers," she concluded, crossing her arms in triumph.

Later I would learn the catechismal release from this scissors hold—that the reverence for Mary was not "worship" from the Greek *latria* but *hyperdulia*, meaning something short of idolatry—but at this stage in my life I didn't know this distinction, so I asked her who she worshiped.

"I only worship the one God who sent his son, Jesus," she responded smartly. At the name of Jesus the three of us bowed, actually nodded, our heads. In the fifties it was common practice to bow the head at the name of Jesus. This gesture threw her off her pace. She wasn't sure if we were agreeing with her, participating in vain Catholic ritual, or simultaneously twitching. I used her moment of indecision to change the subject.

"You're not from around here originally, are you?" I asked.

"No, and I'm not from Pennsylvania neither; born in Tennessee, raised in West Virginia till we moved here."

"Ever think about running away?" Tommy asked. I was surprised at the boldness of his question, but we had assumed she was being held against her will. "Don't you get tired of your father's sermons?"

"That's none of your business, but I'd never run away cause Jesus wouldn't like it." Our heads nodded again, relaxing her a little more. "How about you? You ever think of running away?"

We all laughed at the silliness of the question. "But we're not trapped," said Jimmy.

"Oh, yes you most certainly are," she retorted. "Trapped in worldly pleasures and all your sinfulness."

"We're not trapped in sinfulness. We go to Confession once a week," said Tommy.

"Not gonna help," she said self-righteously. "No priest can forgive your sins, only Jesus"—more nods from us—"can. And He ain't gonna less you turn your life over to Him and say the sinner's prayer. Say it with me now, fellas, you might die tonight."

I thought to myself, *What is going on here? We thought we were going to liberate her from her life of pain and lack of freedom and here she is trying to get us to join her and become holy rollers and give up praying to Mary.*

We three were silent for a moment. Finally Tommy saved us. "No way," he said. "Catholicism is the one true religion."

I looked at Jimmy. "Yeah," I said.

"Yeah," said Jimmy.

"Suit yourself, but if you change your mind don't hesitate to knock on our door," she said. We felt the welcome in her voice even though there were strings attached. She held out her hand. One by one, we shook it, Tommy last. He said,

"It's great," said the three of us at once. "It's like flying," said Jimmy. "It's like parachuting," said I. "It's like going to Heaven," said Tommy.

"Now that I doubt," she said, grinning for the first time.

"Why don't you join us tonight?" I asked, really hoping that she would. "We'll whistle for you."

"Well ... we'll see."

"No, really," I said. "It's not a sin—especially for you. It's your hedge."

She chuckled. "We'll see. I better go."

"Before you do," I said, "I have a question."

"About how to be saved and give your life to Jesus?"

"No, about the privet hedge and our jumping game. Why does your father never stop us?"

This time she laughed out loud. "Well, you know that right on the other side of that hedge is one of the doors with scripture written all over it."

"Yeah."

"Well, my father never stops you because each time you jump you nearly touch the door and he says, 'If that's what it takes to get a Catholic to come close to the word of God then let 'em jump. One of these days they'll get the point.'"

With that, she was back on her bike and down the road, laughing. "'Let 'em jump.'"

And he did let us jump that night, though not with his daughter. We whistled a couple of times but she never showed her face. We watched the curtain, but it never moved.

The jumping was extra good that night, devoid of guilt. We even read the entire door next to the hedge as a way of paying the price of admission to a great ride though the air. Something from Thessalonians about being lifted up at Jesus' return. I dedicated one of my jumps to that pale Christian girl. "This one's for you," I whispered as I spun through the air to the waiting privet of ages, cleft for me, and my cousins.

When I went back to visit later that summer the family had moved away, taking their signs with them. The new family, Catholics, had trimmed the hedge in true suburban style. Our jumping days were over.

*M*y Jersey cousins loved baseball, as did their father, my Uncle Tom. Sitting around the living room on a Sunday afternoon watching the Phillies play, they would outdo each other with facts and statistics. I never understood this fascination, nor could I understand how they could remember all that information.

Besides knowing the facts, my cousin Jimmy was a serious competitor as well. During the week I stayed over in the summer before fifth grade, I saw him play in two games in the Little League field near their house. He played third base with the intensity of a pro and got a hit every time he stepped up to the plate. His real value to the team, however, was motivational. Just watching him maintain his constant patter of encouragement to his teammates and challenge to his rivals was exhausting. Luckily for me, there was more to the event than the action on the field.

Theirs was a well-kept field with a dirt diamond and fairly smooth outfield. Along the baselines were bleachers of backless benches painted green. In front of each bleacher was a team bench. Behind the high fencing at the plate was a cinderblock hut housing the snack bar. Lit by a yellow light which supposedly kept away the bugs, the interior walls were plastered with little posters advertising Creamsicles (orange ice with vanilla ice cream centers), Fudgsicles (chocolatey sherbet on a stick), Popsicles (fruit-flavored frozen confections, usually on two sticks that were supposed to separate the grooved sweet equally, but never did), and Snickers bars which, along with Milky Ways and Three Musketeers, were kept in the freezer, producing treats that would last longer than normal because of the thawing time necessary before they could be chewed.

In addition to these prepackaged treats it was possible to buy "snowballs," paper cones full of machine-shaved ice into which was poured flavored sugar syrup of different colors—brown root beer, green lime, yellow lemon, red cherry, purple grape, and so on.

On the counter was a wide tube full of penny stick pretzels next to a bowl of yellow mustard with a basting brush. One of the great six-cent treats of all time was a lime snowball and a pretzel, eaten simultaneously, sometimes with the pretzel desalted with tongue and teeth, sometimes dipped in the ice. If I had more money than usual—say fifteen cents—I could pace a whole game with treats: snowball for the early innings, pretzel or two in the middle, frozen Milky Way at the seventh-inning stretch, while my poor cousin sweated through the ritual on the diamond.

Just beyond the outfield fence ran a railroad track which carried short freight trains between a distant rail-switching yard and local industries and building supply outlets. A couple hundred yards down the track was an overpass bearing a highway and providing perfect fort possibilities at the tops of the dirt banks that rose from the cement walls on either side of the rails. The caves created by the undergirding of the road above could be used as hideouts for extended games of cowboys and Indians or cops and robbers. Whenever we heard a train coming, however, our game would change to ambush-the-train, and just as it passed below we would run down the embankment as though we were going to board it for purposes of robbery or escape from imagined captors. Ordinarily we would stop at the cement wall above the train and let it pass, unboarded.

~~The~~ ~~we spent a lot~~ of time in the caves daring

~~stones unenthusiastically~~ to the tracks when we heard it coming. As the black engine rolled noisily into view, Jimmy looked me in the eye and challenged, "I dare you, I really dare you this time."

This would be my last chance to prove that I was as serious a player as he; I had to go home the next day.

"Oh, yeah?" I responded with bravado. "I double dare you."

"Double dares go first."

I knew that.

The engine and the first two cars passed. *"Geronimo!"* I shouted, and started down the steep slope. As we approached the critical moment of decision, my father's story about the kid who played chicken with motorcycles until he was killed by a car with one headlight flashed through my mind, and I heard my mother's voice: "Don't give a bad example to your cousins." But then I was airborne, amazed at how much easier it was to follow through than stop and teeter on the wall. I felt my cousins just behind me.

We landed in a car full of bags of crushed stone. They looked like pillows, but they stung my hands and knees on impact.

"Holy mackerel, we really did it," I blurted, my heart in my throat.

Jimmy rolled on his side, head on his hand. "Piece of cake," he responded coolly.

"Piece of cake," Tommy echoed.

The three of us had made it safely, but now the question was, where were we going? As the excitement of the physical reality began to wear off, we began to have doubts about the wisdom of our decision—doubts that we did not openly share right away. The mixture of fear and relief and exhilaration had made us ecstatic and we began to laugh and whoop and slap the bags on which we had landed. Tommy began to sing "I've Been Working on the Railroad," and we joined in. The familiar fort faded into the distance, and we found ourselves passing the Little League park. A few of Jimmy's teammates were playing a slow game of "worksies-up," a system of taking turns when there aren't enough players for teams. The batter saw us and waved and shouted something, the other players turned around and waved, and we waved back. Two of the fielders started running toward us but by the time they got to the fence we were too far along for conversation, and soon the field was out of sight.

Now we were entering unknown territory. My super-ego kicked in. Should we jump off? What if one of us didn't jump and kept on going? Should we wait till we got where we were going and then make a phone call? I felt my pockets to see if I had any change for a pay phone. I felt a quarter and a dime. No problem. Which direction were we going? I looked up at the afternoon sun just off to our left. We were going west. (I had just learned this skill in Scouts a few months before.) I shouted to Jimmy above the noise of the train. "West, we're heading west."

"California, here we come," he shouted back, trying to look brave and adventurous.

"Pennsylvania first," I yelled, not showing off exactly but trying to quell the growing fear in my chest with the fact that we might be leaving his home turf but that we were heading toward mine. I half-expected to see the Delaware any minute.

I looked at Tommy. He was frowning and shaking his head. He mumbled something.

"What's the matter, Tommy? I didn't hear what you

we're going to miss dinner and Dad's going to kill us."

And I'll never be allowed to come and stay over again, I thought to myself, trying to quiet my panic with the knowledge that Uncle Tom was a slow eater.

"Don't worry, Tom, we won't miss supper. There's plenty of time yet."

My words of comfort, not fortified with much belief, helped very little. His chin was beginning to twitch.

"I wanna go home," he bawled, and made a move toward the side of the car. Jimmy grabbed his arm and pulled him back.

Me, too! I thought to myself, but said, "Don't be a sissy, Tom. This is an adventure—like Tom Swift." I had been reading these books recently, borrowed from my grandmother's bookshelf in Pennsylvania.

"It's not an adventure, it's just trouble." His face was getting red.

"Don't worry," said Jimmy. "Everything will be all right. The train's going to stop in a minute and we'll get off."

But it didn't and we didn't. We just kept rolling down the track.

Once the train crossed a road and we passed in front of some stopped cars. Tommy clung to the side of the car and

shouted to the surprised motorists, "Help us, we're trapped
... we didn't mean to do this ... help!" They smiled and
waved back, and the train rolled on.

I cupped my hand over Jimmy's ear so Tommy couldn't
hear me and asked him if he knew where we were. He
signaled back that he had no idea. I felt for the coins again—
still there. Wherever we ended up we'd just call Uncle Tom
and he'd pick us up. We'd apologize and promise never to
do it again. It was not a pretty thought. We were in big
trouble.

The train began to slow down. On either side of the
tracks lay dense stands of scrub oak and dwarf pine. No
phone in these woods. Should we get off now or stay on till
we got to civilization and a phone? Tommy decided for us.
Over the side he dropped and down the ladder. Jimmy and
I clambered down and started running back down the track
after my panicked cousin until he ran out of breath and
slowed down.

"See, I told you," I panted as we caught up and continued walking at a more rational pace.

"Told me what?" Tommy had stopped crying. His
panic had turned to anger.

"Told you everything would be all right."

"Oh, sure. Like we're not still in big trouble, like we're
not going to miss supper, like Dad's not going to kill us." He
was marching determinedly, his face thrust forward, still red,
dirty tear smears on his cheeks.

As we walked, we began to calm down.

Jimmy offered a laugh. "Well, we did it," he suggested.
"We took our own dares."

"Yeah, double dares do go first, after all," I responded.
And then, "Recognize anything yet?"

The sun was moving lower. We were coming up to the
crossing we had passed some time before.

"Sure I know where we are," said Jimmy, a little too bravely. "We were just here a little while ago."

A hundred yards later he stopped. "Uh-oh."

I looked down the track at the cause for consternation.

. . . . f... :.. .h. ..:l.

....

go that way, or we could go both ways."

The whistle of a train caused Tommy to jump up. We all looked down the tracks to see an engine chugging toward us. We stepped back several feet to let him pass. The engine, minus its cars, pulled up and stopped where we were. A grizzled engineer, with grimy hat and soot-smudged face, looked down at us and grinned. "Well, if it isn't the ambushers."

"Hey, mister, which way is the ball field in Runnemede?" Tommy called up.

"Come on aboard. I'll show you."

Jimmy and I looked at each other in amazement. Tommy was already halfway up the ladder. When we were all aboard the train started up, taking the left fork.

"This here's Bob, my fireman. I'm Jake," said the engineer. We shook Bob's hand. Jake's were gloved and busy.

The fireman was older and a little grimier. "You guys are real adventurers. How long you been hoppin' freights?"

"This is our first time. We didn't mean to. Are we in trouble?" whined Tommy.

"Well, I could turn you three over to the police," said Jake. The three of us cast guilty, frightened glances at one another. "But I don't think this track goes to a police station, does it, Bob?"

"No, this track don't. I'm pretty sure."

"So," Jake continued, "I guess we'll just have to take you back to the fort under the highway."

"You know where our fort is?" asked Jimmy in disbelief.

"Oh, yeah. We been watching you boys for the last couple of days almost attacking our train here. Kinda surprised you finally did it, after all those dry runs and false starts."

"So are we, to tell you the truth," I said.

"And we'll never do it again. We promise," chimed in Tommy, relieved that we were somewhat safe but hedging our bet against being kidnapped or turned over to the authorities. I wasn't sure which would be worse.

We were coming up to a road. Jake asked Tommy if he wanted to sound the whistle. Bob lifted him and Tommy pulled the cord proudly. We all waved to the waiting cars. A few moments later things began to look familiar.

"There's the ball field," shouted Jimmy, pointing.

Sure enough, there it was.

"You can let us off, right up here," said Jimmy.

The engine slowed, stopped. We all climbed down and stood back a few feet.

"Thanks for the ride," I called up.

"Both ways," said Jimmy.

"We'll never do it again!" shouted Tommy, as if to remind us of the danger now that we were safe.

"See that you don't," said the engineer. "You could have been hurt bad."

Or killed, said a voice inside me.

I looked at Tommy. His face was streaked with tear mud. "Better wash your face before we go back," I suggested.

We went to the water fountain at the side of the field. Jimmy held the faucet, Tommy washed his face. I watched the engine disappear down the tracks.

"You know what the only problem is with adventure?"

I was a Marian before I was a Christian. My grand-mother enrolled me in the Miraculous Medal Association as soon as I was born and before I was baptized. It cost her twenty-five cents, for which I received a membership card and a blue plastic medal with imprints on both sides. On the front is the likeness of a woman with rays streaming from her outstretched hands to the earth below. Her foot is on a serpent's head and an apple is in the serpent's mouth. All around the woman are the words *Mary, conceived without sin, pray for us who have recourse to thee.* The number *1830* appears below the earth, signifying the year of the vision of Catherine Labouré that inspired the striking of the medal. St. Catherine, a nun of the order of the Daughters of Charity, had meditated on a relic of St. Vincent de Paul, falling asleep as she asked for a vision. She got her wish three nights in a row, ending with an exhortation from the Virgin to have a medal cast with her likeness on the front and renderings of the Sacred Hearts of herself and her son, Jesus, on the back.

Every Catholic child of the 1950s grew up believing that such visions and visitations were possible. Some of us even prayed for such a vision. Actually I was ambivalent about it. On the one hand I wanted a vision; on the other hand I knew that such a vision could kill me. Just like the little match girl in the Hans Christian Andersen story whose vision of her grandmother coincides with her death, I knew that if I saw the Virgin, I might die—either because I was not pure enough to receive the vision and live, or because Mary wanted me to join her in Heaven. Worse than death, how-ever, was the possibility that Mary would give me an earthly task that I would not be able to perform successfully, thus condemning me to the fires of Hell for all eternity. There was a lot at stake, obviously, and even the Rosary couldn't quiet my fear of this fate. It was the improper recitation of the Rosary by the children in Fatima, Portugal, in 1913 that led to the appearance of the Virgin there with the accompanying visions of the imminent world wars, after all.

The Rosary is a chain of fifty-nine beads (each representing a rose in a garland, thus the name), a medal, and a ~~⋯ ⁻⁻ ⁻ ⁻⁻⁻ ⁻⁻ ⁻⁻ ⁻⁻⁻ ⁻⁻⁻~~ of the beads says a different prayer for

allowed me to wear ⁻⁻⁻⁻⁻
myself back to sleep. I usually kept one under my pillow or on my bedpost. It was also good for helping one drift off to sleep at the beginning of the night, especially if one was distracted by the noise of parents' company downstairs or one's sister's pajama parties.

One Friday night in my seventh-grade year I lay in bed distracted by memories of the week just past and thoughts of my sister's friend, Mary Hogan, with her sixth-grade body budding beneath her nightgown as she and Nancy played records downstairs, ate popcorn and potato chips, and drank Frank's Cherry Wishniak Soda with two other less pretty friends.

The week had been complex, to say the least. On the family front, I had been in trouble for a dispute with my sister over the use of the record player. We hadn't come to blows over it, but I had been abusive in my language and was reprimanded by both my parents. I was in the right, of course, and now the music coming from downstairs kept me from forgetting our quarrel.

In addition, school had been confusing. Everyone was excited about a Catholic Senator from Massachusetts, John Fitzgerald Kennedy, running for President. There had been discussions all week about whether it was possible for a

Catholic to be elected. It would be the first time in history if it happened, but I was trying not to get my hopes up.

More confusing than the political issue, however, was a new word we had learned in Cathechism class, a sin against the Sixth Commandment—"fornication." We had tried to get Sister Mary Florian to be specific about the word's meaning but to no avail. She tried to keep us at bay by remarking that it was something we couldn't commit until we were older, but we wanted to know what it was so that we would know not to commit it when we *were* older. Finally, she said it was "being close like married people, only without being married." This still left most of us clueless, since television and movies were almost as careful as Sister in their presentation of sexual intimacy. The only frank talk about sex I had been exposed to had been a session in Dick Kelly's basement with a dirty magazine, but what he described was too fantastical to be true, or even practical, I thought.

All of these memories and ideas swirled in my imagination, making it impossible for me to sleep. I wondered if this might be the night that the Blessed Virgin Mary would appear to take me to Heaven before I was old enough to perform fornication. I suspected I would be too weak to resist the temptation to do whatever it turned out to be; and having succumbed, I would be condemned to Hell for all eternity. I lay there wondering if I should pray for a visit from the BVM, or just say my Rosary without intention and try to ignore the giggling and crackling downstairs, and at least get to sleep so I could get up early the next morning to beat all the women in the house to the bathroom.

I decided to pray for a visitation. I took my beads, and with forefinger and thumb on the crucifix began the Apostles' Creed, then moved on to the other beads, thus quieting the voices inside my head and drowning the sounds downstairs with my recitation.

One of the secrets of the Hail Mary prayer is the breathing pattern that it occasions. Half the prayer can be said on the out-breath, half the prayer on the in-breath. After three decades, the body is calmed and the mind enjoys a kind ... Usually. Not this night, however. I

just like on the Miraculous ...

toward me, stopping at the foot of my bed. I knew it must be very late because there was no sound coming from downstairs and my sister and her friends never fell asleep until two o'clock. My heart was beating hard and I held my breath, waiting to die or be chided for not saying the Rosary correctly or be given a task I would not be able to complete.

"Be not afraid, Edward. I have heard your prayers and I know your thoughts," came the voice.

All my thoughts? I wondered. *Even the impure ones about my sister's girlfriend? I'm going to Hell.*

To change the subject, I asked, "Do you have a task for me?"

A pause, and then the voice said dreamily, "Yes, you must be nicer to your sister. Do kind things for her and her friends, like cook them breakfast. Here is a rosary in honor of my visit."

I felt something drop on the blanket near my feet. I didn't dare move to get it.

"Now I must go."

"Wait," I said, surprised at my boldness, but I wanted to prolong the vision. "Can I ask a question about the future?"

"Yes, you may."

"Will Kennedy be elected President even though he's a Catholic?"

"Kennedy will be elected President if you keep saying the Rosary and resist all impure thoughts." She knew. I knew she knew.

"One more question," I blurted, trying to change the subject again. "Will Russia be converted in my lifetime?"

"If you say the Rosary it will be. Now I must go. Look out your window and you will see me going up to Heaven."

I got out of bed and looked out. I could see her reflection behind me in the hall light. Then the light went out, and I could see the back yard and the night sky filled with stars and a few racing clouds. I opened the window and looked up, assuming she would be going through the roof and on up from there. The wind was blowing through the trees, but I could make out the rustle of her garments. I saw nothing clearly until I caught a glimpse of her disappearing behind a cloud, like the portrait of the Immaculate Conception, only without the cherubs, and then nothing, just the sky. And the stars. I drew my head inside and closed the window. Was this a dream? Or had it really happened?

I tiptoed downstairs to see if my sister and her friends had heard anything. They were all asleep, potato chip bags littering the floor by their sleeping bags. I returned to bed and found the rosary she had left me. Nothing extraordinary, but of course it wouldn't be. The Virgin was a maid of Nazareth, after all, a simple girl. After a few decades, I fell asleep.

My alarm waked me early. I went downstairs to fix the girls breakfast, vowing to be nicer to my sister than I had been. I think they were surprised at my service to them because they giggled the whole time. I didn't once look at Mary Hogan in her nightgown that morning because I would probably have an impure thought if I did, and I really wanted Kennedy to win.

*P*hiladelphia boasts the oldest system of Catholic education in the country, thanks to Bishop (and recently Saint) John Neumann, who laid the groundwork, and to innumerable other bishops who made savvy land deals in the last century, thus making it possible for the Baby Boom of this century to be reflected in a building boom of high schools. Appropriately, the high schools bear the names of these patrons of education. I attended Monsignor Bonner Boys' High School, named for a former diocesan superintendent of schools and located on the grounds of a former Catholic orphanage. The orphanage itself, a massive and beautiful brick building, became a diocesan school for girls, named for Archbishop Prendergast.

Although a small alley, one car wide, was all that separated the two buildings, students from the two schools were never allowed to mingle during the school day. Even the trolley stop was supposed to be segregated. The only occasions where this apartheid was officially lifted was at mixers and Dramatics. Obviously: The Samuel French catalog yields few single-gender plays. In the fall, the Prendergast School would audition boys for its play, and in the spring Bonner High would audition girls for its musical.

In the course of my four years, I auditioned for two of each—and made the cut all four times. Making the final cut was not really a big deal for two reasons: few guys ever tried out for the girls' play, and the chorus for our musical was so large that few guys and virtually no girls were ever cut. My friend John Walsh claims to be the only one who didn't make the Bonner musical, and that was because he was caught off-guard, chosen as the first auditioner when Joe Hayes, the director, suddenly reversed the order of the line he thought he was in back of.

The auditions were raucous, chaotic affairs. The auditioners would sit in the one-thousand-seat auditorium until it was their turn to line up in batches of thirty across the stage. Mr. Hayes would then try to teach us a dance step, and we would all do it together, while Hayes's partner, Ray Gold, would play the music on the piano. Then we would do it individually, starting from the left. If the auditioner were really off the beat, he or she would be asked to sit down. The rest of us would give our names to the stage manager and go home, unless we wanted to try out for the chorus or a principal role. Those who had been cut from the dance audition would be able to try out for the chorus, and if they didn't make that (almost unheard of) they could join Father Spinelli's stage crew. It was usually a win/win situation.

Joe Hayes, the director, was a short, manic man with an overbite and an enormous amount of energy. All during the auditions, and later the rehearsals, he would run up and down the aisles of the cavernous auditorium shouting at us, then onto the stage to physically accost a boy or girl who was out of step or off key, moving the whole time, encouraging, denigrating. His partner at the piano was a calming influence on the proceedings. Gold would sit patiently at the piano, hands in his lap, sometimes nodding wisely when Hayes would address a caustic remark about the cast to him, letting him vent his anger or frustration. They had been working together for a long time, it was clear.

They were hired by Bonner, as well as several other schools in the area, to produce a show that parents, alumni, ⸱ ⸱ ⸱ ⸱ ⸱ of The musicals they produced

me, because it facilitate ⸱⸱⸱ ing girls. There were other places for this quest, but none as nerd-friendly as the Bonner shows. There were football games, but there the focus was on a bunch of other, more athletically prone guys; there were mixers, but the criteria for attention there was also somewhat athletic—skill on the dance floor. The musicals were not demanding, and since the cast was so large, there was always a lot of down time for flirting and making connections in the lobby, or corridors, or classrooms where various subgroups of the cast were stabled until time came round for the specific numbers on stage.

Flirting in a suburban Catholic High School in the early 1960s was not exactly a solo activity. Rarely did one boy try to make a move on one girl without a great deal of support from their respective cliques. More often, entire cliques of boys would flirt with entire cliques of girls. Sometimes these cliques were formal, with sorority or fraternity names. The clique of girls that I was involved with for most of my junior year, for instance, was called Beta Alpha Beta.

My male clique was informal and didn't have a name, until John Rafter, Louie Cataldo and I went underground with "Phi Phi Phi" (fie on women, fie on government, fie on the Church), but that was closer to graduation time, after we had begun to wax cynical in our senior year. In the heyday of interclique dating, we had no formal organization, we were just a bunch of guys from two different parishes that had shared the same trolley stop since grade school. As luck would have it, most of the girls in Beta Alpha Beta were on the same trolley line, so there was ample time for eye-play and elbow-play before and after school.

Of course all contact would stop when the trolley doors opened in front of the schools. Once on school property, no contact was allowed between the sexes. Except at rehearsal.

The intricacies of interclique dating are highly complex, perhaps as complex as language itself. A vital component is body language, individual and group. Imagine two single-gender groups, each with its own pecking order, meeting in the vast lobby of a high school auditorium. As soon as the two groups spot each other, there is a flurry of whispers and wisecracks, posturing and preening. The individuals in each reset their physical relationship with their respective wholes, some subtly hiding, some coming forward, until a diplomatic structure for communications is set up, and contact can be made. If the groups are known to each other, some discussion about pairing off has already gone on, but such a bold step has not yet been taken. Group is dating group, although subliminal forces are already in play. A logical step at this point might be a group visit to the soda shop. After that, one or the other of the groups sponsors a party for everybody, and slowly the process yields more intense subgroups, say three and three go for a triple date, and so on. Although it seems somehow natural to a guy who has been through this process, I suspect that the brain trust of Beta Alpha Beta was very exact and calculating in setting up me, Jim Kelly, and Lou Cataldo with Kathy Hughes, Norma Madden, and Terry Hartnett. It was Kathy Hughes with whom I was finally matched for the prom.

The process leading up to the prom was quite complex. First Beta Alpha Beta had a Halloween party at Nancy Bruner's house. The evening began with a tone of ⋯ ⋯ one danced except in large, noncommital ⋯ ⋯ to be shown, fol-

dance, ⋯ ⋯ ment of furtive hand-holding.

By the end of the evening, the winnowing process was well on its way. It was clear that Kathy and I, Norma and Jim, Louie and Terry had been paired off. Later in the week, phone calls among the sorority sisters would seal the arrangement, after which there was a code of honor limiting contact with a paired-up boy. Breaking the code of honor would result in excommunication.

It was quite a natural grouping, actually: Jim and Louie and I were good friends; as were the three girls. Kathy and Norma, in fact, lived very near each other, not far from the schools, and walking them home became a happy pastime as the school year progressed. We would wait, Jim and I, at the trolley stop at the foot of the path until the girls came down. We would chat at the trolley stop, although we all were on alert for the sight of a white starched tiara covered by a black veil—the dress of the Sisters of St. Joseph—and one particular nun, Sister Phillip Neri, the disciplinarian of the girls' school. If she caught us unawares, the girls would be literally hauled back up the hill by their earlobes to serve the first of many detentions. Although she would be clearly visible for fifty yards or so before she reached an ear, it is a tribute to the focus of young love that so many girls were detained for this offense.

Once we had gone a block beyond the trolley stop, we could talk with impunity though do nothing else—for as long as a girl was in her uniform and a guy in Bonner's jacket and tie, they were representatives of the schools and any behavior unbecoming a Christian Lady or Gentleman could be reported by neighbors and passersby, resulting in punishment for the culprit if identified, or for the whole school if flagrant enough. No hand-holding, no arms around the waist, and certainly no kissing and hugging. Once inside the house, however, it wasn't the neighbors that kept you from touching; it was a higher power.

The rules for heterosexual etiquette among Catholic teenagers of the Baby Boom were fairly strict, in public or in private. The rules that Norma and Kathy enforced on me and Jim were quite clear.

1. No goodnight kiss was allowed on the first date—handshake only, if that, even.

2. A peck on the cheek and a quick run in the house was acceptable on the second date.

3. After that, no kiss was permitted unless money had been spent by the boy on the girl. (This rule seems somewhat crass on the surface. As practiced and perceived in 1963, it was a practical rule—any girl that shared her favors without some kind of gesture from the boy was cheap. No girl wanted to be cheap. Later on, in our cynical senior year, we would be able to go to a hamburger place called Scotty's for a fifteen-cent hamburger and a ten-cent Coke and immediately proceed to the quarry behind the park. No one would feel abused, the minimum requirements having been taken care of.)

4. Making out (a.k.a. "Makking") could take place after three dates, but only if the participants were fully clothed.

⌐ ┌───┐ kissing was allowed only if you were

Dry kisses, no tongues. ... ── ─
body part by the hands. And of course, no unclothed body parts.

This mixture of innocence and desire made the school year a wonderful one for me and Jim Kelly. After walking Kathy and Norma over to Norma's house, we would be invited in (if we were lucky) for a Coke. Norma's mother worked and didn't get home until 4:30, giving us about two hours for couch wrestling. Norma lived in a large house with a big living room that had an enormous couch—big enough for two couples to cuddle comfortably, for two glorious hours of pre-pre-pre-foreplay. As I look back, I am in awe of my adolescent attention span and my patience with the rules.

Years later, when I learned about the medieval tradition of Courtly Love with its rules set up by Andreas Capellanus under the direction of Eleanor of Aquitaine, I understood them completely, at least in their origins. Norma and Kathy's rules were every bit as strict. And we were obedient. Kathy's uncle was the superintendent of Catholic Schools, and both sets of parents were pillars of the Catholic community. We didn't ask for more—we would have never succeeded.

Nor would we have really known what to do with it if "it" was available to us. We didn't even know what the varieties of "it" were. The television still had active censors at this time; one foot was still on the floor in bedroom scenes at the movies, and we only went to movies that had a good rating from the Legion of Decency. If we wanted to go all the way, the thing to do was date Jewish girls, it wasn't a sin for them, they didn't believe in Heaven anyway.

The belief in an afterlife of punishment for sin and reward for virtuous acts influenced much of the behavior of Bonner boys. Nineteen hundred and some years of Catholic thought had resulted in a theology of Mortal Sin that was clear and powerful. Mortal Sin resulted in being condemned to Hell for eternity, unless you went to confession before death and received absolution from a priest. Venial Sin did not condemn one to Hell but still had to be confessed lest one spend time in Purgatory.

The centuries of debate in learned Latin that are behind this kind of thinking are somehow forgotten when one looks at the oddness of the conclusions. In 1962 it was thought to be a Mortal Sin to eat meat on Fridays or miss Mass on Sundays. Guilty of either? Go to Hell. No exceptions, unless you (a) wore a certain kind of cloth medal called a scapular around your neck, (b) went to Communion for nine First Fridays in a row, (c) were truly sorry for your sins but were kept from confession by a fault not your own, and so forth. Besides meat on Fridays and missed Mass on Sundays, the other great Hellward aspect of life was sex. And it wasn't just premarital intercourse that resulted in eternal damnation: any overt act of stimulation outside of marriage—and even inside of marriage those acts that did not lead directly to the possibility of procreation—could lead to Hell. Even impure thoughts. Orgasms always, though nocturnal emissions were exempt, as long as they weren't really enjoyed.

High school religion classes at Bonner were exciting when the issues of sin and sex were raised. One of the best aspects of the old school of Catholic education was the kind of legal thinking it engendered and nourished. Discussions of doctrine often ended with the priest against the wall claiming, "It's a mystery of Faith," when the doctrine wore thin on the abrasive washboard of logic and common sense. . . . and Hell, when the touchstone of

speakeasy . . . .

persons thus discovered. Anonymity is normally assured, thanks to the darkness and denseness of the screen—sometimes wire, sometimes plastic. After an initial prayer by the penitent and a report of the length of time since the previous confession, the sins are listed and questions are asked about the circumstances and frequency. In the case of sexual sin, the most common question asked by the priest, besides number of times, is "Alone or with others?" After the report comes an assigned penance, usually recitation of prayers, to be said after the event, and then an Act of Contrition, recited while the priest says a prayer of absolution while blessing the penitent.

At Bonner, there was a line outside each of the side doors of the confessional, and the people standing behind you knew how long you were inside and thus had some idea of the severity of your sins. If you wanted to be forgiven a sexual sin, you chose Father McBride. He would forgive anything. His line moved very quickly. Choosing your priest was a secret of success.

In a system like this, of course, it is important to have as little time possible between the sinful act and the absolution of it. Since most parishes had confessions on Saturday afternoon, it was a good idea to have the sinful date on Friday night. A sinful date on Saturday night would mean a week's wait until the sacrament, and the possibility of accidental death during that time was frightening. There was a legend circulated, I suspect by the priests and nuns, about a couple who had engaged in heavy petting, thus committing a Mortal Sin, and driving home they were hit by a train, died, and both went to Hell. In my sophomore year, a Prendergast girl actually was beheaded by a runaway freight car two blocks from the school, lending this genre of horror story a certain amount of credence.

Not that Kathy Hughes and I were ever in danger of the pangs of Hell from our Makking Marathons. No tongues, no touch, no torture—at least not in Hell.

Though the Monsignor Bonner Junior Prom wasn't held until April, the process started in January when Father Hartmann, the class moderator, named a committee to select a band, a place for the after-prom party (and a second band for that event), and finally, a theme. The committee chose for the prom proper the Al Raymond Orchestra, a large group of older tuxedoed musicians who played big band music. Since this choice would give the event a classy tone, the committee had the liberty to choose a wild band for the after-prom party.

For that event, they chose The Revelers—pronounced "Revaliers," with an inexplicable accent on the last syllable— a quartet with guitars and drums who specialized in current hits. The site for the party was the Falcon House, a catering hall two miles from the school. Since the theme for the prom was "Camelot," in deference to President Kennedy, the unofficial theme for the after-prom party was "Dance-a-lot."

And we would. Until five o'clock in the morning. This closing hour was actually a safety measure, a result of a fluke in the Pennsylvania Motor Vehicle Code nicknamed

"Cinderella." This act rendered sixteen-year-olds' drivers' licenses invalid between the hours of midnight and five A.M. Thus, on some level, the law required that we dance all night.

On Friday morning, the day of the prom, the Augus-̶ ̶ ̶ ̶ ̶ ̶ ̶ ̶ ̶ ̶ ̶ ̶ who ran the school held an assembly in order

the First Amendment, so they live, get home safely, and then the boy discovers something "down there," some kind of pimple, and goes to the doctor and is diagnosed as having syphilis, which means the girl is called in and has to name names, and the investigation is horrible and costly and complex. The moral wasn't about using protection but about not going all the way, because the consequences take time and are embarrassing. It didn't really affect us in the way it was supposed to, beyond reinforcing the supposition that girls were dangerous and had cooties.

There was never any danger of "going all the way" in the car on prom night for Kathy and me. Even if she hadn't been the niece of the diocesan superintendent, we would have had little opportunity since we were triple-dating.

After school Louie and I helped Jim clean his father's station wagon. Then we went to Saul's Tux Rental to pick up our tuxedos, for which we had been measured a week before. These rented tuxes never fit well, but the design was so different from our school clothes it was hard to tell. On the way home I stopped at the florist to get Kathy's corsage, which I put in the refrigerator as soon as I got home.

I was ready at six-thirty when Jim and Louie arrived in the station wagon. The logistics of the event were simplified by the fact that all three of our dates lived in the same neighborhood. Kathy's house was the last stop. The other two couples came with me to the door, since her mother wanted to take pictures of all of us. Mrs. Hughes answered the door and led us into the parlor at the foot of the stairs, chatting with the girls about how nice they looked while I stood with my eyes fixed on the upstairs hall.

Suddenly there she was, pausing a second before making a regal descent. She looked beautiful. Her pale pink semi-formal gown, buoyed up by yards of crinoline which hid her legs above her knees, was waisted by a green satin sash. She laughed nervously as she descended, balancing on green high heels dyed to match her sash. Her hair had been professionally set and stiffly curled, making her seem taller than usual but not taller than me, I was relieved to see when she got to the bottom of the stairs. The top of the dress was prim and proper—no exposed shoulder, no cleavage, just enough freckled skin at the throat to be Catholically daring.

"Here's a corsage," I blurted, handing her the box. It was a wrist corsage, the kind she said she preferred, saving me the horror of pinning a flower to her bodice in front of her parents. She lifted it out and handed me the box so her mother could help her with the corsage. I was useless, trembling with excitement and hormones. When the corsage was in place, it was time for pictures.

"Now line up, everybody, let's get a group shot first," said her mother, as Mr. Hughes fumbled with the flashbulb. The six of us obeyed, clumsily.

"Closer together, everybody, I want to get you all in," said her father, squinting through the lens. As we inched together, her perfume filled my nostrils, and my trembling increased as I faced the dilemma of what to do with my hands. Should I put an arm around her, hand on her waist? Should I hold my hands clasped in front of me? Boldly I went for her waist, not grasping it but touching it gently. I held my breath. The camera flashed.

"Hold it right there, I want another," said Mr. Hughes, rewinding for a second shot. Another flash. "Now one of

were both proud and surprised

been transformed into such gentlemen, dressed, escorted, and on our best behavior.

The gym was decorated with cardboard castles and tin-foiled arches, with lots of crepe paper and ribbons. The large mirrored ball in the center of the rafters was put to work, the first time I had seen it revolve since I came to the school. The music was the music I had grown up with at home—Glenn Miller, Tommy Dorsey. Kathy and I danced every dance but three or four, separating only for the traditional meetings in the ladies' room and visits to the refreshment area in the cafeteria downstairs. A good time was had by all, as the school newspaper would report a week later.

Then it was off to the Falcon House for a light dinner and more dancing, though of a different type. The Revelers were cooking that night, taking only three breaks in five hours. "You Can't Sit Down" was their theme song, a hard-driving fast dance tune that they played continuously for one full hour between 3:30 and 4:30, to our exhausted delight. It became a marathon challenge for some of us, but one that we were equal to—Kathy and I took only one break. The last half hour was all slow dances, though most of us merely stood and held one another, shifting from foot to foot.

At five o'clock sharp the party was over. Jim's license was valid again, and we piled into his car. He dropped Kathy and me off in front of her house for final goodbyes and promised to return to pick me up. I told him we were in no hurry.

Few mornings have found me so awake so early. The light was perfect. The prom had been perfect. We stood on her front steps for a long time, looking at each other, our arms around each others' waists, without words, with long (dry) kisses. An amazing social process of winnowing and wooing had brought us to this place. Never again would we demand so little of each other and provide so much. No sin was committed. Grace abounded. April 17, 1963, six-fifteen A.M.